A TAIL GUNNER'S TALE

A TAIL GUNNER'S TALE

Gerald E. McDowell

VANTAGE PRESS
New York • Los Angeles

FIRST EDITION

Copyright © 1991 by Gerald E. McDowell

Published by Vantage Press, Inc.
516 West 34th Street, New York, New York 10001

Manufactured in the United States of America
ISBN: 0-533-09100-4

Library of Congress Catalog Card No.: 90-90112

1 2 3 4 5 6 7 8 9 0

*To all of the air crews who flew with the
Eighth Air Force during World War II and the
fighter pilots who gave all of us comfort
with their vigilant support.
We all are indebted to those who gave their lives
during this conflict and helped make it
possible for everyone to live as a free people once
again.*

Contents

List of Plates

Preface

In 1943 the air war over Germany and Europe reached its peak.

Hundreds upon hundreds of B-17 Flying Fortresses pounded Germany daily, with hundreds of German Luftwaffe fighters meeting the challenge.

These devastating air battles brought about many stories from air crews who survived harrowing experiences daily. But thousands did not survive.

This is the story of one such crew as seen through the eyes of a Flying Fortress tail gunner: how they trained, how they flew, and how they met the enemy head-on in battle and eventually were shot down over enemy territory after only eight missions.

After a spectacular 200 mph crash landing, the entire crew spent eighteen months as German POWs until the end of the war.

"Hell's Belle" crew. *From left to right, top row:* Bert Stieler; top hatch gunner, radio man; Harold Wingate; top turret gunner, engineer; Charles Guinn, pilot; John Hinda, right waist gunner, armorer. *From left to right, center row:* Kenneth Fallek, copilot; Robert Hornbeck, navigator; Sidney Edelstein, bombardier; Charles Dyer, left waist gunner, engineer, *From left to right, front row:* Bill Rasmussen, ball turret gunner, radio man; Gerald E. McDowell (author), tail gunner, armorer.

Crew of the "HELL'S BELLE" Flying Fortress
A/C #23060
Eighth Air Force
91st Bomb Group—401st Squadron
Bassingbourn Airdrome
near Royston-Herts
England 1943

Pilot . . . . *.Lt. Charles A. Guinn*
Copilot . . . . *.Lt. Kenneth W. Fallek*
Navigator . . . . *.Lt. Robert J. Hornbeck*
Bombardier . . . . *.Lt. Sidney Edelstein*
Top Turret Gunner . . . . *.S/Sgt. Harold E. Wingate*
Ball Turret Gunner . . . . *.S/Sgt. Bill E. Rasmussen*
Top Hatch Gunner . . . . *.S/Sgt. Bert A. Stieler*
Left Waist Gunner . . . . *.S/Sgt. Charles W. Dyer*
Right Waist Gunner . . . . *.S/Sgt. Cecil Comer**
Tail Gunner . . . . *.S/Sgt. Gerald E. McDowell*

*Replacement for original gunner, John (NMI) Hinda, grounded due to frostbite. Hinda flew as part of of the original crew except for the last mission.

A few POWs in Stalag 17-B, adding on to each other's work, wrote the following ballad.

At that time, I copied it into my "Wartime Log," as did others, but I have no idea who the authors were.

I was told then that there were more verses, even other versions. But I never saw them.

However, I have included this one with the text, as I feel it sets the stage for what you are about to read.

THE BALLAD OF BOLT STUD BILL
(authors unknown)

Now there's some who say that a gunner's pay is altogether too
 high.
But that ain't so 'cause we all know we earn it when we fly.
It's a rugged game and there ain't much fame, life at its best is
 short.
For the men who dare to fight in the air for the Silver Wings
 they sport.
Now I'm going to tell of a tale of hell, of guts and an iron will.
Of the war in the sky of the men who fly and the 25th raid of
 Bolt Stud Bill.
Now Bill was one of those gamblin' sons, he had the lust for
 the game.
Cards, roulette or any darn'd bet, to Bill it was all the same.
He couldn't tame his lust for the game, he'd sit in every darned
 night.
He'd draw his pay and there he'd play, till time for the morning
 flight.
And if Bill couldn't be found dealing "stud" on the ground,
Or in the barracks couldn't be seen,
He'd be crouched by his guns dealing death to the "Huns"
 from the tail of a B-17.
He learned all his tricks in group 76,
The outfit had taken abuse.
For every raid made to the Jerry we paid the price of a couple
 of crews.
Then into the group replacements would troop eager for mis-
 sions to face.
They'd make just a few, and then a new crew would fly in and
 take their place.

It got pretty bad and a bunch of the lads were discussing the
   problems one night.
While taking long sips from a bottle's tips they proceeded to
   get a bit tight.
One of the guys considered quite wise, a mathematical slick,
With paper and pen and a drink now and then promised the
   problem he'd lick.
With glasses of Scotch they sat round to watch an anxious
   bleary-eyed lot.
"Slick" sweated and swore and cussed the Air Corps till finally
   his answer he got.
I've figured it out and there isn't a doubt no matter how you
   strive.
I'm willing to bet there's none will get through mission 25!
And there in a daze through the cigarette haze sat Bill with a
   drink in his hand.
He listened awhile then sort of a smile came to his homely pan.
"Slick" damned near choked on the words Bill spoke, the room
   suddenly went still.
"I have a hunch there's one in the bunch, so I'll take that bet,"
   says Bill.
"I'll tell you what let's make a pot, come on boys let's chip in.
I'm willing to buck on my gambler's luck that I'm the one
   who'll win."
There's no mistake, the odds were great, but the lure of chance
   was strong.
So one by one, in their dough they flung, each thought he
   couldn't go wrong.
It was early spring when they started this thing and when sum-
   mer rolled around,
Left of the men, there were only 10, the rest were all shot
   down.
Bill always thought of the bet they made that cursed fatal night.
And he'd sometimes say in a troubled way, "It looks like Slick
   was right!"

But still he flew though well he knew, the fickleness of fate.

Then he'd think of the dough and off he'd go another raid to make.

He howled and moaned in a dreary tone, he swore he'd fly no more.

And in this way he found one day that he'd finished 24.

But the combat game demands a price that all must pay who fly.

This settled fare you can't escape and pay you must, or die!

For such is the law of the E.T.O., there's no exception to the rule.

And so Bill knew before he was through he'd paid his debt in full.

His weight was down to a hundred pounds, he walked like a man in a daze.

He had a blank sort of look, his hand it shook—

He was changed in many ways.

The Purple Heart, the DFC, the Silver Star had he.

Bill had made his 24th raid, just one more to go free.

He was sweating it out, this one more bout, holding out for an easy one.

And there happened by chance a raid to France, that looked like it was a milk run.

The briefing was done and the morning sun was coming up in the East.

They cleared the props and pulled the chocks and took off for La Pallice.

Bill sat in the tail, watched the vapor trails, as over the channel they flew.

And he thought of the bet and the dough he'd get when this last mission was through.

They carried the sight on this last flight, for they were leading the way.

The hours passed and they came at last to where their target lay.

With anxious eye Bill scanned the sky, no fighters could he see.

But the sky was black with bursting flak as they reached the old I.P.

When out they swung on the bombing run their course was level and true.

They were flying by the P.D.I. when the target came into view.

Bill's brow was wet with clammy sweat as they opened the big bomb bay.

From the nose he could hear the bombardier as he shouted "Bombs away!"

Bill glanced at the time and spoke thru the grime, we've hit the target at noon.

This is the easiest run I've ever begun, but he spoke a little too soon.

For the plane gave a lurch and a downward plunge like a craft on a heavy sea.

Well, I guess this is it, for we've sure been hit and it looks pretty bad to me.

And to his dismay when the smoke cleared away, Bill saw that two engines were out.

When from the waist in a tone of haste he heard a gunner shout,

"Don't worry 'bout 'flak' cause were falling back and there's fighters coming in fast."

Right then and there Bill breathed a prayer as the first Focke-Wulf flashed past.

He tightened his grip so his guns wouldn't slip and settled down to fight.

His shoulders slouched in a gunner's crouch between his twin gun sights.

The big guns bounced and bucked in their mounts, spewing forth their leaden death.

As he swung his guns on a diving "Hun" that was coming in fast on the left.

Bill's eyes were bright with a burning light, his lips were set in
a grin.
The twenties flashed with a bursting flash as the fighter planes
came in.
In a streak of red the tracers sped, Bill knew his aim was right.
For a German plane in a burst of flame blew up within his
sights.
Through barrages of flak and fighters' attack the big ship stag-
gered on.
Still in control tho' shot full of holes, and two of the engines
gone.
Up in the front the pilot slumped with a bullet through his
head,
In the waist of the ship with a shattered hip lay a gunner dying,
the other dead.
Shot in the thigh with an attempt at a sigh, Bill croaked in a
bloody spray,
I've lost the bet but I'm not through yet, come on you "Huns"
and pay.
In they came, guns aflame like hornets from their nest.
And well Bill knew from the way they flew they were Herman
Goering's best.
Through the tracer's flash and the cannon crash he heard the
copilot shout,
In a cracking tone on the interphone the order to bail out.
Bill saw at a glance he hadn't a chance, his luck had passed
him by.
For their gallant plane was a coffin of flame, it was hit the silk
or die.
The engineer, the bombardier, were the first to hit the chute.
And the rest of the crew that were able to, quickly followed
suit.
With screaming dives the sky was alive with Jerrys swooping
to kill,

And hating to quit tho' he knew he was licked the last to leave was Bill.

Out Bill came from the burning ship like a human Zephyr on high.

He grabbed for the ring and found the thing as he tumbled through the sky.

When your life depends on odds and ends of silk and cords and such,

Right then and there he breathed a prayer, cause his life wasn't worth much.

He twisted and turned and oh how he yearned, and the Devil laughed at his plight.

But a PFC at home, you see, had packed Bill's chute just right.

With a yank on his back up went the slack, in his chute he started to sway.

He glanced all around and heard not a sound, for the planes had flown on their way.

Below him lay the Bay of Biscay, he knew he was in for a swim.

There broad and black and covered with white caps, the bay awaited to greet him.

Bill had lost his bet and had many regrets, for the coast was far out of view.

And England's shore he'd see no more, his life was just about through.

Bill should have quit like his old pal "Slick," then he would have been safe at home.

But he lost his way in the cold bleak bay and went down beneath the foam.

Men can't understand when fate takes a hand that the odds against them are great.

Now Bill was in trouble and went down for double, but his luck turned out to be fate.

Now if some still say that a gunner's pay is altogether too high,

Just think of Bill and his iron will and his last battle in the sky.

A TAIL GUNNER'S TALE

Chapter One

After being sworn into the regular Army on January 8, 1943, I left one week later for basic training at an induction center at New Cumberland, Pennsylvania. After several days of that, I could easily see that the Army way of life was not for me. So, with a friend who felt the same way, I went to the C.O. and managed to get transferred to the Army Air Corps (as it was known in those days, it didn't officially become the Air Force until 1947), and then we were sent to Miami Beach, Florida. Here was the beginning of "military discipline" and fundamentals. We drilled on the drill field day in and day out for hours each day, just like regular foot soldiers. After a few weeks of this, I shipped out to Apalachicola, Florida. Here there was more training and on one day, a trip to the range to fire the 30/06 rifle—fifteen rounds at 150 yards. After scoring fifteen bull's-eyes out of fifteen rounds, I suddenly realized what I had done and for a moment wished I hadn't, out of fear of being picked as a sniper in the regular Army. As a young lad I practically cut my teeth on a rifle, so this was no real challenge to me. But nothing was said and soon after that I shipped out to Lowry Field, Colorado. Now the "real" stuff began with more military discipline and various techniques, all for the purpose of training me as an airplane armorer.

Technical training was given at an adjoining base named Buckley Field. There we schooled for weeks at night from about 8:00 P.M. to 5:00 A.M., emphasis being on .30 and .50 cal-

1

iber machine guns, turrets, aerial cannons, both 20mm and 37mm, bomb racks and shackles, high demolition bombs and all other types—plus pyrotechnics and various types of machine-gun ammo. In addition, we also covered the basic electricity of the plane's turrets and bomb rack shackles: in general, everything about the firepower of the airplane. I really felt like I was going to college.

When the course was finally finished, I learned that as a result of high grades, I had been selected along with two others in the class to go before the Board of Review as a prospective ground armament officer. However, it was not to be. The electrical questions in the oral quiz were misinterpreted by me, so I lost my chance and a first lieutenant's commission, I later learned. So I continued on and left for Tyndall Field, Florida, the main training center for aerial gunners. It was located about fourteen miles southeast of Panama City, along the coast of the Gulf of Mexico. Tyndall Field was the largest aerial gunnery school in the country. You didn't simply become a gunner by asking. Requirements were high just to enter. You must not be over 5'10" tall and not weigh over 170 pounds. Vision must be 20/20 and free from color blindness, and muscular coordination and focus must be perfect.

Good average intelligence and sound nervous system are also required. There is no place for a nervous, trigger-happy guy who doesn't know when to hold his fire, or one who can't make up his mind. Training here consisted of firing the big .50 caliber machine guns from turrets mounted on the rear of military trucks at a moving silhouette of a Messerschmitt fastened to a jeep traveling around a controlled track at about 30 mph. The distance was about one hundred yards. Other days, standing on the back of a truck in a large horizontal ring which was about waist high, we went around a special course at about 35 mph firing shotguns at clay birds. These birds were shot out of a trap at different angles, one at a time, each time the truck reached a designated point as it traveled around the course. Truck speed started at 20–25 mph and was gradually increased each day until it reached 35–40 mph. We all found this more fun than anything.

Emphasis was now being placed on "leading" the target for the air-to-air firing program coming later on. We also fired half-size machine guns, loaded with air rifle shot and powered by compressed air, at small metal enemy planes on a continuous belt along a small embankment. The planes went by like sideshow targets, in which you got three shots for twenty-five cents on a .22 caliber rifle. This showed your "hits" in the dirt as you zeroed in on your target. All of these things had a purpose for aerial gunnery as we all soon learned.

Next came the flying and aerial target practice. I boarded the rear cockpit of a North American Texan AT-6 one bright, sunny morning. The canopy was kept open, front and rear, for this training program. There was a steel loop in the floor and a heavy web belt, which I ran through the leg straps of my chute harness to keep me from falling out during any maneuvers. Proper adjustment was to leave just enough slack to rise up on my toes—now I was ready! My pilot was a lieutenant from Philadelphia, Pennsylvania, who assured me I was safe with him, for he had never left anybody "up there" yet!

We taxied out to the takeoff position and waited. The signal came from the tower and with a mighty roar we headed down the runway full throttle, the pilot slowly pulled back on the stick, and shortly we were airborne. There was a deafening roar to that AT-6 engine as the propeller blades slapped at the air and we climbed upward into the blue morning sky, heading out over the Gulf of Mexico. Soon we were at about 3,000 or 4,000 feet. Far below us lay a number of floating targets in the form of the letter "X," painted white so they could be spotted in the water. Suddenly, the pilot looked slightly over his shoulder toward me and pumped his arm up and down, pointing downward at the targets below, which was my signal to get set—I was!

Suddenly we peeled off and dove toward the targets below, our speed ever increasing as we went. What a sensation as the plane suddenly drops sideways rapidly, and you roar in toward the targets. As we made the first pass at over 200 mph, I opened fire in several short bursts and blew the target to pieces. Up we came in an ascending roar to line up for another pass. As we did, the pilot yelled over the roar of the engine, "You sure blew that one to hell!" Down we went again, roaring over the target as I blazed away, blowing it to pieces. A few more passes were made at different angles and altitudes, with the same results. Bear in mind that I stood up and faced the rear of the plane, shooting over the side at these targets, which I felt added to the difficulty of scoring. Even so, I had a very good pilot who tried his best to give me a good target on every pass, which certainly made me look good.

So now we headed back to the base, ending another phase. As we approached the field on the downward leg to land and the air speed dropped just below 90 mph, a Klaxon horn went off, scaring the living hell out of me. I felt sure something had gone wrong with the airplane and got ready to bail out. However, I learned it was just a warning horn for training pilots to let them know that the air speed had dropped below 90 mph, but the pilot never told me to be ready for it.

Next came the "air-to-air" firing. This proved to be more difficult. We flew out over the Gulf of Mexico once again, this time to find an AT-6 towing a target made of mesh wire. About one-quarter-inch of the nose of our .30 caliber ammo tips was dipped in colored paint. Each gunner had a different color paint on the tip of the ammo so when the target was hit it would leave your color ring around the bullet holes, which was how your daily score was determined. After one week of aerial firing, a high percentage of "hits" was required in order to pass.

I dare say I can't recall just what the percentage was after all these years, but I do remember it seemed high, just to qualify.

The planes we used this time were the Lockheed Ventura B-34 and the A-29 Lockheed Hudson, both medium bombers. The A-29 was used extensively by the RAF for bombing missions and by us for Ferry Command. This phase of air-to-air firing went on for five days, and scoring was kept for each gunner. As luck would have it, on our fourth day out, one burst I fired hit the quarter-inch towing cable, severing it, and the target went down in the Gulf of Mexico, giving every gunner on board zero for the day! As you can imagine, the other gunners were upset with me for costing them the day's score. Fortunately, we had learned our training well earlier and with the next day's score, each of us had more than enough points to pass this phase.

Besides delivering supplies to Britain with the A-29, the Ferry Command delivered huge numbers of these bombers to the British on the Lease Lend plan for their use in the war with the Germans.

I almost washed out as an aerial gunner when we flew in these mediums for gunnery practice. The pilot was good, but a real "cowboy." He flew like he was "barnstorming" in the 1930s. As we flew along in the clear morning sky out over the Gulf of Mexico, I awaited my turn to climb into the rear turret as the pilot scanned the sky for the tow plane. I was sitting just in back of the pilot's compartment with my two belts of .30 caliber ammo. Care in aiming would be essential to scoring as the belts were purposely short, about fifty rounds each. I saw the tow plane some distance off to our left and flying in the opposite direction. Once we were far enough past the tow plane we were to turn and come back, making a pass and firing at the target. I had just noticed the air speed was 220 mph when our plane suddenly stood up on its left wing and we went into the tightest banked turn you can imagine. The air speed dropped instantly to 190 mph and the centrifugal force glued us all to the floor of the plane.

In the middle of the turn, our instructor signaled me to go back to the rear turret and load up for firing. I could barely stand up, and the belts of ammo felt like they weighed fifty pounds. I had only taken a couple of steps to the rear when the plane suddenly leveled off, instantly relieving the centrifugal force, and I almost threw the belts of ammo up to the ceiling of the plane. Recovering, I made my way to the turret, loaded the guns, and I was ready. I fired short bursts as we passed the target, feeling confident of my aim, and was certain I had scored. Then the smell of burning powder and burning paint from the bullet tips, plus the heat of the sun in that turret, began to turn my stomach. Also, while I was turning the turret in one direction, the pilot went into a steep banking turn in the other direction, again! This time as I looked up through the plexiglass dome on the turret, I saw a medium-size vessel going by in the waters of the Gulf, which could only mean we had rolled over in another one of the pilot's "cowboy" maneuvers. In any case, when I left the turret I had to head for the bucket and heave. I really believe this pilot did all of this on purpose, not only to show off, but to sort of initiate us like the "new kid" on the block. Besides, I got the impression before this phase of flying was over that these pilots didn't like hauling us around for target practice—they wanted to be off flying by themselves.

The next day we went up in the A-29 bomber again, but this time I fired from the waist guns instead of the rear turret, which helped my stomach some. This pilot was much better but the maneuvers were still too much for my stomach, and yes, I got sick again!

Now I was beginning to worry because my instructor citing a requirement , reminded me that if I got sick and heaved during the next flight, that would be my third time and I would be washed out of gunnery school.

Well, the next day we went up in a B-34 Ventura bomber, which seemed a little bigger and heavier. Our fifth and last flight, and I made every effort not to get sick. I remember moving around a lot and swallowing hard as we neared the end of the flight, trying my damndest not to heave. Another student flying with me kept trying to help me by saying, "Not yet, Mac, not yet! Just hold on a little longer! We're almost there! We're almost there! Just a little more!" Well, I didn't think the wheels would ever touch the runway, but they did, and I headed for the bucket. I saw by the bucket that I wasn't the only one to use it. The rules were if you used it, you cleaned it! So I did but I didn't care; the wheels touched down before I got sick, so I passed! Not only that, but I was awarded the Marksman medal for my total score, even though one day's firing on the target had gone down in the Gulf of Mexico.

Even so, I was concerned about this apparent chronic air sickness. I had originally hoped for fighter pilot training but was unable to take some of the preliminary ground tests without feeling ill, and my depth perception was off some. So now I was hoping for a gunner's spot on a medium bomber, which I obviously couldn't tolerate either. After talking to a flight surgeon about the problem, he explained it would require an operation on the inner ear canal, to which I said no. He then replied that I could probably get assigned to heavy bombers and the high altitude would probably be more favorable to my condition, since they were smoother in flight. So that eventually brought me to the B-17s.

In the days following, there were more calisthenics, day after day, on a course that took a good thirty minutes to cover. There were all the usual things: rope climbing; horizontal ladders to swing across, which seemed to pull my arms out of the sockets; wall climbing; and the toughest of all—the large horizontal logs, too big to get a grip on, so I had to swing across hand over hand. My wrists felt like they were pulling apart. The purpose of this was to strengthen the wrists so you could pivot those big .50 caliber guns (seventy-nine pounds each) quickly—and it did!

June soon rolled around, and it was time for graduation. We all got our silver gunner's wings and sergeant stripes. I was proud to learn later that I tied second highest in my class. So now I was ready to put my training to work, but before this came a trip to Seattle, Washington, for a brief stay. All I seem to remember about Seattle was high-altitude flying and shooting tow targets out over the Pacific Ocean.

In a few days, along with other gunners, I was sent to the air base at Moses Lake, Washington. Moses must have been the only guy who could tolerate it there. It was just a dry desert basin, with mountains around the perimeter. But this was a training base where crews were put together to train and fly with each other and in different crews, until somebody decided who would be assigned to which crew permanently. Here is where I met the other crew members who eventually made up our permanent crew.

As part of our high-altitude training, a new type of oxygen mask was issued to us and about four of the crew members I had been with at the time, along with some other gunners, filed into the decompression chamber. The large door was closed and sealed, and everyone strapped on their oxygen masks. Slowly the pressure was evacuated from the chamber until we reached the equivalent altitude of 38,000 feet, where we remained for a time. Some of us managed to qualify for flights up to 38,000 feet in the normal atmosphere with just the oxygen mask. I never knew of any missions higher than 30,000 feet, but as always, they wanted to see how much you could take. A few men had to go to the outer chamber and be returned to ground-level pressure because of the fierce pain when they got the "bends." Suddenly my buddy, John Hinda, doubled up and fell from the bench to the floor in agony, holding his abdomen.

As they carried him to an outer chamber to return to ground-level pressure, I suddenly felt as though I had been stabbed with a white-hot poker in the back of my left hand. It would be thirty minutes or more before they could lower the pressure again so when they asked if anyone else wanted to go down to ground level, I jumped up, yelled "Yes!", and headed for the outer chamber. My pain was gradually increasing and although it was nothing like John's pain, I didn't know how it would be thirty minutes from now. Sealing the door of the chamber, it was like a crash dive in a submarine. One man I could see outside the chamber spun the big wheel of the pressure valve furiously as the instructor kept yelling to him, "Take it down, take it down, faster, faster!" By now my head felt like it would explode from the pressure as it increased in my ears. I just couldn't swallow or "crack" my ears fast enough to keep up with the increasing pressure. We were falling in excess of 18,000–20,000 feet a minute, according to the pressure gauge I saw.

Just as I felt like the top of my head would come off, we were suddenly pressurized again and in a few seconds everything was okay, except John had to be attended to a little. That seemed like a harrowing experience to me because you don't normally return to ground-level pressure with such furor, but then this was an emergency. In any case, we had been at high altitude long enough to pass the test for high-altitude flying.

Then too, if you had any loose or bad fillings in your teeth, the drastic difference in pressure would usually pop those fillings out.

Having finished a training phase at Moses Lake at the end of July 1943, our crew was given a one-week furlough plus a three-day pass. So I headed for home to see my folks and a girl I had. I knew this would be the last I would see any of them until the war was over, that is if I made it back okay. It was the shortest ten days I ever remember. But time awaits no man, so

9

on the ninth day of my leave I boarded an American Airlines DC-3, as there were no jet airlines in those days. My destination was Pendleton, Oregon, and from there I would find my way to Walla Walla, Washington air base, our new assignment.

As we flew along, I began to wonder if we would ever reach Pendleton. It was dark for more than half the trip for we had taken off from Philadelphia, Pennsylvania, near dusk, only because I had wanted to stay home as long as I could. We flew through a couple of sizable electrical storms, and the lightning kept dancing all around the plane threateningly as the thunder clapped loudly. We pitched and rolled like a galleon on the high seas and I sure wished I had been in that B-17 instead, with its four engines; then we could have climbed high out of that mess. I felt nervous in that thing with only two "fans" to keep it up. Arriving many hours later at Pendleton, I caught a train to Walla Walla and went hunting for some familiar faces from the crew I was with at Moses Lake, to see if they had all gotten back from their leave. Some of them had and the others showed up the next day.

Up to this point, we had not yet met our pilot-to-be, Lt. Charlie Guinn. He had several different crew members training with him at the time and although a few of us were in other phases of training, our paths had not yet crossed. The copilot, navigator, radioman, and I had not yet been assigned to that crew, nor did I know any of them at that time either.

Lt. Guinn had been flying and training as a B-25 pilot when it was suddenly decided they needed him and many others to fly the B-17 Flying Fortresses, so he was transferred to heavy bombers and the 396th B.G. at Moses Lake for a crew assignment and training.

Originally Guinn had been assigned a crew at Moses Lake in July of '43 before we all went on leave. However, upon our return to the 88th B.G. at Walla Walla, this was changed on

August 6 and the four of us I just mentioned were assigned to him, replacing the others already on the crew.

If you did not like your assignment or some other member of the crew, this was the time to speak up and it could probably be changed somehow; otherwise it would remain "as is," for this looked to me like it would be our "permanent" crew!

Our crew seemed comfortable as we were so no changes were requested, as far as I know. However, one thing did come up. I had qualified as a first armorer at graduation, as did my friend John Hinda. But only *one* first armorer is assigned to each crew and John was already assigned to Guinn's, so I was to go elsewhere. So, once again I went to the C.O. with John, and I agreed to accept the position of assistant armorer so we could stay on the same crew. I asked if my rank and pay would stay the same and when he said it would, I thought *who cares then.* There are always two armorers on the ship and the assistant armorer is the tail gunner, so that is how I became a tail gunner. The first armorer is made a waist gunner. Actually, this was a plus for our plane to have *two* first armorers on the same crew.

About four B-17s were at Walla Walla; they had been brought in just for the various crews to train in. Everyone arriving there had been well-schooled but we all needed to fly and train as crews to become effective. But with only a few B-17s on hand, we didn't fly every day.

Soon we were assigned a B-17 for training, so as a new crew, in a strange plane, we started to train together and get acquainted.

We did a bit of night flying at Walla Walla, too, with a little training course on night vision, with a red shield fully covering our eyes from about midafternoon on. Once it was completely dark, the shields were removed. On one of these nights we went over Walla Walla and as I sat back there in the tail, I thought the city lights seemed kind of close, even the big neon signs and lighted billboards were vivid. But I decided it must just be a clear night or my night vision course made it easier to see. The next day, the Commanding Officer had all the pilots fall into formation announcing that he had had a call from the mayor that one of our bombers had "buzzed" the city the night before. He promised that if the guilty pilot would step forward and take his medicine, that would be the end of it right now. Naturally, no one stepped forward. So the C.O., determined to get the guilty pilot, immediately fined every pilot in the unit fifty dollars! Now, fifty dollars out of a second lieutenant's pay in those days was a bit of money!

Forty-five years later at our reunion I brought the subject up to Charlie Guinn, our pilot, asking him if he remembered that incident. Looking around very innocently, he said, "Yeah, I remember that; now who do you suppose that could have been?"

I said, "Oh, my God! You don't mean that was us?"

"Yep," he said.

I began laughing and shaking my head in disbelief. In all those forty-five years, the thought never crossed my mind even once that we were the guilty ones. But we had roared across the business district with full power and full superchargers at about 300 feet. As we passed through a residential section where Lt. Guinn had a girl, the vibration broke some 40–50 windows. This was confirmed later at another base, but they never did learn who did it.

Walla Walla was also the base where our navigator was checked out by plotting a course and then we flew it. This showed the navigator's ability to plot a triangular course several hundred miles long, then bring us back to the base at an E.T.A. (Estimated Time of Arrival). Our navigator did well on the day runs, but one night we flew far to the southwest, took a new heading for Reno, Nevada, then another heading to bring us back to the base at Walla Walla. Somehow, there was an error and we got lost over the Black Hills of the Dakotas. The radio went out, like it regularly did, and we were in trouble. After what seemed like several hours of flying and no signs of ground beacons, the situation was critical. The pilot came on the intercom and said, "We're running low on fuel so I'm going to make a 45-degree right, and if we don't see something soon, we'll have to give this airplane back to the taxpayers."

Sometime during all this, Bert, our top hatch gunner/radio man, also fearing the worst, decided to "drop the ball." This is the antenna with about a ten-pound ball on the end to stabilize it when it is reeled out. It can be run out about 200–300 feet, so one had to be careful as it could possibly catch on something below. Also, it should only be used in an emergency and on "Emer-Freq Voice," as it is called. The problem otherwise is that it broadcasts on all bands at the same time, overriding everything else. But this was certainly an emergency.

A short time later, Bert made contact with Mountain Home, Idaho. Passing this on to the pilot, we took a new heading for a time and suddenly there were runway lights below. I sure let out a sigh of relief. It was pitch-black and I didn't know how I would ever have mustered the courage to bail out, should the engines have suddenly quit. The Black Hills were below, and no telling what the outcome of a parachute jump might be under the circumstances. Then, too, it was very cold there now and the chances of being found were just about nil, it was so dense and thick with trees for miles and miles in all directions.

It was now the wee hours of the morning as we made our approach and landed, coming in on the "fumes." We taxied in from the runway, and as the engines wound down to a halt, we all let out sighs of relief. There were some B-24 Liberators based there and we also saw some B-29 Superfortresses, which explained the 1 1/2–2 mile runways. Mountain Home was one big air base. The personnel there were very cordial and realized our predicament. This was a real treat for many of them who had never been close to a B-17, judging by all of the questions and excitement. They fed us all and bedded us down for what was left of the night.

Mountain Home had notified Walla Walla as to our whereabouts, so early the next morning we had breakfast, they tanked us up, and we took off for our home base. Our arrival was not a welcome one, especially for our navigator. The pilot got some hell since he was responsible for the aircraft and the crew, but the navigator was the one who really got "chewed out," up one side and down the other, for his gross error. We had needlessly burned up some 800 gallons of gas due to his mistake. So to say the least, there was some real "butt" kicking going on for a while. A short time later the navigator was required to set up another flight on a similar triangular course of several hundred miles, and believe it or not, our navigator missed our return E.T.A. by just a few seconds.

Leaving Walla Walla, we soon arrived at Madras, Oregon, for another phase of training. Taking off a couple of days after our arrival, we flew out over the desert at treetop level and into the gunnery range, blasting every target on the desert floor as we passed. Our score turned out very well for the crew of gunners, but no wonder; we covered it at an altitude of around *100 feet!* Now picture this in a four-engine bomber with a 103-foot wingspan. It was rough as a cob flying at this level, but Lt. Guinn said afterward, "I wanted my gunners to get a good score!" It was difficult controlling the plane, too, judging by the back of his shirt, which I noted was completely soaked from perspiration.

Later, for some reason we were sent out in the desert to do some low-level bombing on some troops with ten-pound bags of flour. I gathered these troops were on maneuvers, and they just wanted us to acquaint them with the roar of airplane engines overhead and simulated bombing. These sacks of flour exploded when they hit the ground, showering men and equipment with flour. Some hit the personnel, too, so we were suddenly not very popular around there.

Another day, flying at about 21,000 feet altitude, our bombardier did his stuff over the practice range with 100-pound practice bombs, doing quite well, as I remember. Flying toward the target range, we reached the IP (initial point), then made our turn to begin the bomb run. At this point, Lt. Guinn made every effort to keep the needle at dead center on the PDI (pilot's directional indicator), thus flying the airplane straight and true. Meanwhile, the bombardier lined up on the target and locked the controls of the plane to the bomb sight, announcing on the intercom, "Okay, Chuck, I've got it!" From there on the bombardier actually flew the plane with the bomb sight, making any adjustments needed. After the usual "Bombs away!", control was returned to the pilot.

There were high mountain ranges around Madras, so we had to use the practice range at the Walla Walla air base.

Following this, we had some tow target practice out over the Pacific Ocean, flying high and blasting targets with our .50 caliber machine guns. On one occasion, we towed the target so the gunners on other planes could have their practice.

Another thing I had studied as a gunner which I forgot to mention was the Renshaw system of aircraft recognition.

In a darkened room, aircraft we would encounter in the combat zone, both friendly and enemy types, were flashed on a screen, approaching at different angles. Some came in groups and we had to give the number of planes in the group. Others were pictures of single aircraft and we had to identify each one. Constant training gradually taught us to recognize them in a split second. This program was excellent, I thought, since it would go a long way to help us in not shooting down "friendly" aircraft, yet removing any doubt in our minds when we did see a "Jerry." Too many RAF planes were fired on, some hit, due to their similarity to the Luftwaffe planes. Each day of class the speed of the slide projector's shutter was increased to train our eye, starting at 1/25th of a second and slowly increasing each day. The day of the written exam, the speed of the shutter was 1/100th of a second, with some slides even at 1/200th of a second. The big thing to learn about this was not to blink your eyes for a few moments after the image disappeared but to continue to stare at the screen. Doing this, the image seemed to remain on the screen for a bit. Our instructor taught us this, apparently for use in combat.

I think it should be noted here that each aerial gunner had a second job on the plane. Normal procedure was as follows:

Top Turret Gunner—Engineer
Ball Turret Gunner—Assistant Radio Operator
Top Hatch Gunner—Radio Operator
Left Waist Gunner—Assistant Engineer
Right Waist Gunner—Armorer
Tail Gunner—Assistant Armorer (except in this case I was also a first Armorer, as explained on pages 8 and 9)

Training appeared to be complete and we were ready to start toward our P.O.E. (Point Of Embarkation), which begins the trip out of the country, then overseas. We will remain a B-17 crew now! Thank God for that, after all the training we had together.

There were many things about the B-24 Liberator that were in my opinion "bad news." My training covered B-24s also, and I was quite concerned that I might be assigned to one. The B-24 flew a little faster, but was much trickier to fly and control. Those I saw in flight constantly dipped up and down like riding a roller coaster and, as I recall, drifted some, too. Even the best pilots seemed unable to fly a tight formation with them, and this was a must for your own protection. However,

I am sure there were many crews who thought they were great, but it just wasn't for me, considering what I had learned and observed.

Over 18,000 B-24 Liberators were built, the highest amount of any bomber produced by the United States, which was about 6,000 more than the B-17 Flying Fortress production.

With the B-17 Flying Fortress having been dubbed "Queen of the Sky," Fortress crews were filled with pride about their aircraft and its capabilities. Many of our B-17 crews riled the B-24 Liberator crews when we told them, "B-24s were built from the crates the B-17s were shipped in!" But they had their "digs," too, and got back at us, all in fun, of course.

The B-17 had much better manners in the air, and consequently was much smoother and easier to control. It also flew about 5,000 feet higher and was far better in combat. The Luftwaffe, when given the choice, would attack the B-24s every time. They could never take the punishment of the B-17 Fortress. The wing of the Liberator was relatively weak and too often if hit in crucial places, it would give way and fold up. Then, too, one hit on the hydraulic line of the tail guns knocked out the power to the turret. With power lost to the turret, they had to be hand-cranked! Now picture that in the heat of battle. This shortcoming alone, which I had learned in armament school, told me right away that as a gunner I wanted to fly combat in a B-17 Flying Fortress. Many crews flew the B-24s, it is true, but I didn't want to face combat in one of them. The B-17 had two electric turrets, each with an individual source of power. My guns in the tail were mounted together on a pivot and operated manually, as did all of the other guns on the ship, so power there was not a problem.

It's easy to see why the B-17 Flying Fortress is continually proclaimed the greatest war plane of World War II. In 1985, the Flying Fortress celebrated her fiftieth birthday! Sadly, there are only ten left flying in the world today. Nine of these are here in the United States and one in England. Those flying here are privately owned by groups, flying organizations, and even some individuals who have them just for the love of the airplane and flying. These people fly them to air shows all over the country. Pride of ownership, I would say. There are often films on television and articles written regularly about this dramatic airplane. For all of its beauty and grace, nothing has ever come close to its ruggedness in battle, and with its firepower, brought so much frustration to the Luftwaffe in combat. All of us who flew in B-17s are very proud to have been a part of this magnificent airplane.

Somewhere around this time, we spent some time at a base in Salt Lake City, Utah. For some reason, I can't remember just what the training was. I would guess a change of equipment for overseas duty and more flying and general "sharpening" up. Of course, there were numerous places I had been earlier in the program and some afterward, but with forty-five years having gone by, I doubt if I will ever recall all the bases or what training I had there. I do have the most important parts of the training mentioned although a couple may be out of order.

We finally reached our P.O.E. (Point Of Embarkation), which was Scott Field, St. Louis, Missouri. We stayed there for a few days getting some changes in our "gear" and other things for the flight overseas.

During the few days of waiting for our orders, there was not a whole lot to do. One day, Charlie Dyer's girl came to the base to visit him, all the way from Spencer, Indiana, just to see him one last time before we left for overseas. Charlie climbed into the trunk of her car and left for a day or two. Lucky for him he was not missed, as we had all been restricted to the base and, as I recall, put on ready alert. My, isn't love a wonderful thing. After the war when Charlie came home, he married that girl and they raised a wonderful family.

Soon after this, our orders were cut on September 27, and we were ready to go.

Chapter Two

Upon leaving the country, some stops were necessary before actually crossing the ocean. First was Syracuse, New York, for a day, then Presque Isle, Maine, where further orders of October 4 transferred us to Gander, Newfoundland. This, I believe, was about October 11, 1943. We stayed here just a few days. I saw some B-24 Liberators painted white for submarine patrol and several British Hawker Hurricane fighter planes. The Hurricane pilots looked like schoolboys, but then I guess we all did. They sure could fly! I watched three of them as they went roaring down the runway in a "V" formation. As they reached flying speed, they swayed the control "stick" from side to side a little, which bounced the wheels on the runway slightly. This in turn caused the plane to become airborne sooner, and as soon as the wheels didn't touch any longer with this movement, the pilot snapped the landing gear up. It seemed the plane was almost sitting on the ground for a moment, then the pilot hauled back on the stick sharply and disappeared into the heavens.

We soon had clearance and one night at 10:00 P.M. we cleared the props, pulled the chocks, and took off for Ireland. I sat right by my guns the whole trip over, keeping a watchful eye out for submarines. Word had it that there were subs with radar often surfacing and shooting at passing aircraft—having downed some! The ice-cold Atlantic in the middle of the night wasn't for me, so I wanted to be sure to see them *first!* My guns were loaded and kept ready. I never did see any signs of a sub on the whole trip.

As I sat there and the hours rolled by, I listened to the roar of the engines as I gazed at the moon's reflection on the ocean waters. I began to think about the good old USA, home, friends, school, and many things in the past, wondering how long it would be, if ever, that I would see them all again.

We were flying at about 24,000 feet and on oxygen most of the trip. Suddenly, the wings began to ice up and the deicer boots would not clear them, as the ice was too thick. So we had to drop down to about 1,000 feet, where the warmer air would clear them. Now it seemed like we were skimming the whitecaps.

The next morning, October 15, the coast of Ireland appeared and I heard someone say on the intercom we would be landing at a place called Nutts Corner. It took us ten hours to fly here from Gander, Newfoundland. Actually there was an error somewhere, as we were supposed to land at Ipswich, England. Nutts Corner was in reality a radio beacon, but did have an emergency landing strip, if needed. As we arrived, I noticed a few other B-17s that had already landed. So, not knowing of the "error," I presumed this was a landing point for incoming combat bombers for distribution to various groups in England. We taxied off the runway onto the apron, cut the engines, and the props slowly came to a stop. As we jumped out of the plane, an American "noncom" ran over to our plane, wringing his hands, and with glee shouted, "Boy, are we glad to see this. We lost sixty yesterday!"

He was no doubt referring to the very heavy losses of the day before, October 14, the day of the *second* Schweinfurt, Germany raid in which another sixty B-17 Fortresses were lost. Rass had just jumped down to the landing strip and when he heard that, he spun around, grabbed for the doorway as if to climb back in the plane, shouting, "Let me get back in this thing!"

Later we left there and headed for The Wash on the coast of England. Once we were billeted, everybody seemed to relax

21

with what was left of the day. The next day, our crew took a truck down to the coast and fired .50 caliber machine guns out into The Wash to learn more from watching tracers and how you could lead the target. Then we tried firing the Thompson .45 caliber submachine gun, which during Prohibition was known as the "Chicago Typewriter." This was done so we could get the feel of it and be able to use it. On board the airplane, however, the gunners carried .45 caliber automatics as sidearms, and I believe our officers had a .30 caliber carbine or two. Then suddenly G-2 advised against carrying arms. Should you be shot down and shoot someone during your escape, the penalty if you were caught would be prison for sure, maybe death!

Our original orders had been for us to go to a base somewhere in England where a new group was being formed, known as the 401st Bomb Group. However, after the onslaught of a few days earlier in which those sixty B-17s had been lost in the second Schweinfurt raid, our orders were changed. So after several days of just waiting at The Wash, we were sent to the 91st as a replacement crew. This was on November 7. On the ninth of November, we began several training missions to get familiar with group operations, their procedures, and formation flying in combat missions.

The 91st was the most prestigious group in the Eighth Air Force, located at USAF Station 121, Bassingbourn Airdrome, near Royston-Herts, England, and operating during the period from September 12, 1942, through June 23, 1945. During that period, the 91st Bomb Group (H) was known as the "Ragged Irregulars." The first mission was flown on November 7, 1942, and the last mission on April 25, 1945.

Following is quite an impressive record the 91st Bomb Group compiled during its operations in England.

- The 91st Bomb Group flew a total of 340 missions, employing 9,591 B-17s, and dropped a total of 22,142.2 tons of bombs on European targets.
- The 91st Bomb Group destroyed more enemy aircraft (420) than any other group in the Eighth Air Force and sustained the highest loss of B-17s (197).
- The 91st Bomb Group was the first to attack a target in the Ruhr—Hamm, Germany, on March 4, 1943.
- The 91st led two famous missions against the ball-bearing works at Schweinfurt, Germany (August 17 and October 14, 1943).
- Was also the first Eighth Air Force group to complete one hundred missions—January 5, 1944.
- Was the first group to test "flak" suits—March 1, 1943.
- The 91st Bomb Group had the first B-17 to complete twenty-five missions without a casualty—"The Memphis Belle."
- The 91st also flew the B-17 "Nine-O-Nine" that completed more missions than any other bomber in World War II without an abort—140.
- The 91st Bomb Group received two Distinguished Unit Citations for their achievements on the missions to Hamm, Germany (March 4, 1943) and Oschersleben, Germany (January 11, 1944).

There were four squadrons that made up the 91st Bomb Group: The 401st, 322d, 323d, and the 324th. We were assigned to the 401st.

Many famous B-17s came from this group, I learned. Widely known and written about yet today are the *Memphis Belle, Nine-O-Nine, Shoo Shoo Shoo Baby, Royal Flush,* and *Eagles Wrath,* just to name a few. It was a long-established group and its crews were considered very stable and staunch, with top efficiency. We were about to become part of the 401st Squadron of that famous group.

I thought Bassingbourn was very impressive and mighty-looking with all of the B-17s standing around. Seeing this sight, I could feel for the first time the reality of this as the "real thing"—and combat was not far away.

I found England to be a very quaint, homey place. I liked it from the very beginning and often wished I'd had the chance to see more of it.

I was quick to notice that the group had a mascot, too. It was either a golden retriever or an Irish setter, as I recall, named "Redline." When a military person had his pay held back for some reason, either shipping out or charges due for equipment replaced, a red line is drawn by his name and pay is withheld until charges or transfer is completed. "Redline" never received any pay, hence the name. A very unique thing about this dog was that no matter how many airplanes flew over our base, American or British, bombers or fighters, he never looked up until a B-17 flew over, then he would gaze skyward at it for a few seconds.

After checking in, we learned that we had been assigned to a brand-new airplane, which had been taken from another crew that had just arrived with it. This of course they didn't like one bit. It was too new to have nose art yet, so the last three digits were its designation—"079."

When I got back to the barracks, everyone was milling around getting acquainted with the other flying personnel and checking our quarters, bunks, etc. For some reason a crew member from either the *Royal Flush* or the *Eagles Wrath* turned to me and asked, "Is that right, you're a tail gunner?"

I replied that I was and asked, "Why?"

He said, "Never mind, you'll find out!"

Well, find out I did. I learned that more than one tail gunner had been flushed out of the tail of a B-17 with a fire hose when the ship returned from a mission. But, back then I never knew that the tail gunner had the most dangerous position on the airplane, either. I took those losses to be the "breaks" of combat and prayed I wouldn't be one of them.

A few days later our crew went up together on a routine flight, except that our copilot, Lt. Fallek, gave up his seat to a captain who was flying that position as "checkout" pilot. It was the captain's job to throw switches on or off, make radical adjustments in the various controls, and generally "screw up" the airplane to see how quickly our pilot, Lt. Guinn, could recover the ship to normal flight. Once he even cut an engine out on our left wing, then shortly afterward cut it back in. Almost at the same time, he cut another one out on the right wing, all to see if Lt. Guinn would lose control of himself or the ship in trying to recover. But Charlie was a very good pilot and everything went smoothly. All of these maneuvers, of course, were to try to simulate "hits," which under combat conditions would affect the operation of the equipment greatly. It may even render it useless, requiring skill in hopefully recovering control of the airplane and continuing on.

During all of this, Lt. Fallek had decided that since he had given up his seat, he would take a nap on the lower deck in front of the pilot. Spreading out his fleece-lined jacket, he made himself comfortable and soon dozed off. When that first engine cut out, he raised his head with a start and peered out through the plexiglass nose, watching the prop slowly wind down to a halt. Wondering how the other engines were doing, he rolled over to look out, just in time to see the second prop slowing to a halt, not realizing the first one, which was behind him, had been restarted at the same time. Instantly, he bolted up to the flight deck with, "What's wrong, Chuck, what's wrong?" By now we were laughing at his reaction, then he suddenly caught on.

With the checkout over, we headed back to the field. Two other B-17s were flying in the formation with us. I was riding back in the tail and as we neared the field, the other B-17s seemed to suddenly pull up sharply and turn away to the left. Studying them, I was puzzled by their action until I realized that they were flying straight on and we had fallen away from them and were now peeling off and sideslipping into an approach to the runway. I was not supposed to be in the tailgun position when landing, but since nothing came over the intercom, I now felt I should stay put so as not to change the balance of the plane by moving up to the waist. I cringed a little as we made our approach as it looked like we were going to bury one wing in the runway. But this captain was an excellent pilot and we suddenly leveled off, dropped into the glide path, and made the final approach, touching down just as smooth as silk. Whew!

Soon we were on combat-flying status and ready to do our part. Naturally, everyone on the crew was apprehensive, knowing our next mission was perhaps just hours away—and it was.

The following day, November 18, we took off on a mission, but I just can't recall where. All I remember is what happened shortly after takeoff. We roared down the runway, lifted off normally, and when we reached about 1,500 feet, we suddenly hit a "thermal draft" (air pocket) and the ship started to drop like a rock. All four engines began to roar wildly, trying to get a "bite" on the air as we dropped straight own and out of control. There is nothing a pilot can do in this situation except keep fighting for control and hope that the ship will grab "solid" air before it hits the ground! We were just free-falling through the air. At 700 feet, we suddenly hit "solid" air and it felt like we would go through the floor of the airplane. My ammo belts flew out of their 500-round containers and were strewn all over the floor. A couple of the other gunners had the same problem. I felt as though I was in an impossible situation. There was no way for me to get those big, heavy belts of .50 caliber ammo back into their containers in "ribbon candy" fashion. It was almost a two-man job even on the ground. My worst fear was not being ready when it came time to tangle with the "Jerries." Other crew members were having similar problems, as loose equipment of all sorts had bounced off the ceiling of the plane and was strewn about everywhere. The minutes passed as we all tried to recover somehow. I struggled with my ammo belts as we continued on.

Before long the word came down to "call back" the mission, due to weather conditions over the target. Was this ever music to everyone's ears. So back we went, grateful for the outcome of that one. Also, very grateful that we pulled out of that 800-foot drop in that thermal draft!

On November 19, the next day, I believe our mission was a uranium mine in Norway. Two hundred fifty B-17s had been assigned to this mission. Taking off from Bassingbourn, we headed for a rendezvous point just north of our base, where there was a beacon. As our group approached the point, there were suddenly other groups arriving at the same time, instead of the usual intervals. Many were flying at treetop level, while others spoke later of actually hitting some high fences and posts and dragging debris with them on the tail wheel. The situation was extremely dangerous with 250 airplanes flying at various levels, all trying to prevent a midair collision. We were flying at about 1,000 feet ourselves.

As I looked upward through the plexiglass window at my position, I saw groups of B-17s flying in about every direction of the compass as they passed overhead at different altitudes. There were even some planes passing under us, which I guess were the ones tearing up fences. Obviously there was a foul-up somewhere, as we should never have all arrived at the beacon at the same time. It was a miracle that there were no collisions.

Some groups, including ours, finally formed up and headed for Norway. Just how many returned to their bases, I cannot say. We had gone well up into the North Sea when Lt. Guinn realized we were low on fuel as a result of all that flying in circles earlier trying to form up. Consequently, we would never make it back after the mission, so we had to turn back and return to Bassingbourn. *Hell's Belle* had been very hard on fuel for quite some time, and the ground crew for some reason could not correct it. As it turned out, the mission was a "call back" anyway because of the number of "good" people who were down in those mines, rather than just Krauts. This was apparently learned as a result of a coded signal sent to the lead squadron and passed on down to the formation. But then, tomorrow is another day!

On November 24, our mission was Stuttgart, Germany, which was well-known as a real hot spot. With an overcast of heavy clouds, we had climbed to 23,000 feet and were ready to head for Germany when Charlie once again noticed we were already low on fuel and turning back was a must. Electing to turn back and drop down below the overcast where less fuel would be consumed, we gradually descended, breaking through the cloud cover only to run into another problem: the barrage balloons over London! Of course each balloon emitted a warning "beep" signal, but they were of little value since we were right in the midst of them. To make matters worse, there was fog over London at the time, which made it a real zigzag game dodging those steel cables supporting the balloons. They would certainly shear a wing off if hit. Directly, a couple of British Spitfires were on the scene, looking us over very carefully. Had we not given the countersign for the day, they would no doubt have attacked our plane, intending to shoot us down. Then Lt. Guinn, through hand signals, indicated we wanted to get down and away from those balloons and land. So the Spitfires escorted us out safely and even back to our base.

On the twenty-fifth of November we took off on another mission, but I must say it has been too many years ago to remember where!

On the morning of November 26, we were kicked out of the sack about 4:30 A.M. I mention this to emphasize the time required in preparation and flying time needed to reach the target at the best time of the day for us. After breakfast, it was briefing time. Everyone scheduled to fly the mission and the standby crews were in the ready room. It was a closed room with no windows and an MP on each side of the door preventing anyone from entering or leaving while the briefing was going on. Up went the roller shade covering the map of England and Europe. The red yarn around the pins on the map plotting our course into Germany showed our target for the day to be Bremen! A number of groans arose from the group at the sight of this. I guess they had been there before!

After all the details were covered, altitudes explained, and who would fly lead group, high group, and low group positions, small groups of each religion formed with a chaplain for a moment of prayer. Following this, other details were then discussed among just the navigators, pilots, and bombardiers in their separate groups. All of us gunners left at this point and headed for the storage room, where our .50 caliber machine guns were stored. Naturally, every gunner took care of his own gun or guns, cleaning them, making any adjustments, and in general keeping them in perfect operating condition. After all, who would want someone else to care for his weapons when his very life may depend on them!

Each squadron in the 91st readied seven aircraft. Six were to fly the mission and the seventh was on standby at takeoff time in case of mechanical failure or sudden illness of a crew member on one of the other planes. Crews were not normally broken up when a problem arose. Instead, the "problem" aircraft and its whole crew "stepped down" and the standby ship took its place. Perhaps mixing crews did not go well in combat due to the feeling that the unity was not there with a "broken" team —I don't know. But I do know all crews were superstitious about flying in an airplane other than their own and considered it a bad omen.

Soon we were armed and ready to go. Standard bomb load at that time was eight 500-pound high demolition bombs, along with twenty 100-pound incendiary bombs. For some reason, we only carried ten 100-pound incendiaries this time. Although the bomb bay did not have enough shackles to hold this many bombs, the 500-pound bombs were hung normally in the shackles and the incendiary bombs were attached to the shackles in clusters with baling wire.

Just as a point of interest, the 500-pound high demolition bombs were designed not to go off under 500 feet when dropped from the air. This was due to the fact that each one had a threaded propeller device on the nose and an arming wire through it, so that it would not be unwound accidentally. However, the incendiary bomb did not have this device; it just exploded upon impact. Before reaching the "bomb run," the arming wires were pulled from all of the propellers manually, usually by our engineer, whose top turret position was near the bomb bay. After the bombs were released, the small propeller device would unwind from the air currents and fall away from the bomb, exposing the detonator. So if no "delay" had been installed, it would explode upon contact.

The signal was given and down the runway we went, headed for the wild blue yonder and Bremen, Germany. This raid to Bremen was the first 1,000-plane raid over Germany made by B-17 Flying Fortresses. Soon we formed up over the Channel, which seemed to take forever. But then, there were hundreds of airplanes from various groups all over England joining up to form a number of combat wings. Usually there were four squadrons to a group and three groups to a wing.

Each wing covered an expanse of 3,000 feet of altitude, with each group of the wing in a combat box stagger "vertical wedge." This was the ideal battle formation, which utilized the great defensive fire power of the Forts and also provided maximum mutual protection.

We flew "high group" on this one and I believe our altitude was 25,000 feet. The temperature was 55 degrees *below* zero and these were not the pressure cabins of today; we flew in the open atmosphere in those days and it was cold like you wouldn't believe!

Sometime before approaching the coast of Europe, Lt. Guinn announced over the intercom, "Alright, everybody clear your guns!" With that, we all fired a short burst and each position reported back over the intercom, "Waist clear! ball turret clear! tail guns clear!", etc. This was done because climbing to high altitude will freeze the condensation that forms on and inside the machine guns as the plane climbs into the freezing temperatures of the upper atmosphere, making the guns inoperable. So before it reached that point, we always "cleared" the start of the freezing by firing our guns at about 10,000–12,000 feet, which frees the bolt and allows the sub-zero lubricant to do its job. Once that is done, they will stay clear while you are up there in the "deep freeze." I can easily recall how both of my guns always had a light coating of frost on them at high altitude. But then, any of the metal on the airplane seemed to have a frosty look about it at those temperatures.

In fact, all gunners wore a pair of close-fitting pure silk gloves under the heavy fleece-lined leather gauntlets. Should removal of the gauntlets become necessary to work on the machine guns at high altitude, the silk gloves were a lifesaver. Touch that gun anywhere with bare hands and you would leave the skin from them on the gun! This made me think of when I was a kid and was talked into touching my tongue on my sled runner. Every kid had done this, I'm sure.

Reaching the coastline of Europe, we were now flying steady at 25,000 feet and the usual 55 degrees below zero temperature greeted us.

Oxygen was an ongoing problem at high altitude. There were malfunctions, leaks, and worse yet, destruction by enemy gunfire or flak. In some cases, a hit on one of the eight supply tanks would cause an explosion, virtually destroying the airplane. Thankfully, the tailgun position had dual oxygen systems, which were needed should flak knock one out or gunfire shoot one away, which was sometimes the case. Our early oxygen system levels were adjusted manually by the user and could easily be neglected as the plane rose. The pilot would inform the crew over the intercom of changes in the altitude, and we would adjust our dial accordingly. However, the moisture from your breath could freeze quickly in the neck of the "breather bag" and cut off the oxygen supply, which of course you wouldn't know. This was a constant danger so the crewmen had to watch each other for telltale signs of passing out because you could never feel it coming on. This was a concern to me back in the tail position, as no one could see me behind that little closed door.

Some men were affected by the lack of oxygen below 18,000 feet, and all men above that. At 25,000 feet and higher, the lack of oxygen could be fatal in a few minutes. So a new "demand" type oxygen system was introduced, which automatically supplied the user as needed when the altitude increased.

Also, the new oxygen system did not have a breather bag, which was what always iced up gradually on the old one, cutting off the oxygen supply. I often wondered how many average citizens gave any thought to the temperatures we endured or that we constantly used oxygen masks when flying above 10,000 feet (Air Corps regulation).

As for warmth, under our flying gear we did wear an electric suit. This was wired up much like an electric blanket and plugged into an outlet near your station in the plane. Electric gloves were worn over the silk gloves and plugged into the suit at the wrists, and the gauntlets fitted over the electric gloves. Electric lightweight boots plugged into the suit at the ankles, and very heavy fleece-lined leather boots fit over these. Although this did not really keep you warm, it did keep you from getting so frozen you couldn't function properly in those sub-zero temperatures.

The usual combat air speed was 155/160 mph. (Cruising speed was 160 mph.) Although this was a 300 mph aircraft, the slower speed was used so that anyone losing an engine for some reason could still keep up with the formation and not end up a "sitting duck" for the Luftwaffe. Bombers falling back were easy prey for them and were quickly attacked and shot to pieces. Likewise, any loose formations would also attract the Luftwaffe like a magnet.

The sky was clear and cold, and we were all tense as we roared on to the target. As we crossed the Ruhr Valley, the "flak" began and remained quite heavy for a time, then suddenly stopped. This was our signal to expect a fighter attack any minute now. As we waited, the sudden roar of a B-17's engines caught my ear and our plane gave a hard lurch to one side. I got just a flashing glimpse of a B-17, which seemed almost on top of us. I thought, *My God we are hit!*, but no!, we were flying smoothly again. At this moment, our pilot yelled over the intercom to the copilot, "Hey, Fallek, that son of a bitch took all of our goddamned wing!"

Looking out toward our left wing, I saw where we had been hit by that B-17 coming up through the formation. He seemed momentarily out of control, probably from turbulence or trying to change position in the formation, and rammed us, tearing through our wing as he went. His props chewed up about fifteen feet or more of our left wing, narrowing it a good bit as well. I could see cables and wires hanging down and either fuel or hydraulic fluid dripping out of one line. I really felt uneasy at the sight of the damage, especially since we were just heading into Germany. No doubt the rest of the crew felt the same way, but somehow we had to stay with the group to survive. Turn back now, and we would be "dog meat" for the Luftwaffe.

German fighters had been rather light, but the flak was now heavy again. Had the fighters seen this incident, we probably would have been jumped by them as a "cripple," but this was a flak period and you don't have fighters and flak at the same time, for obvious reasons. The trim tabs were adjusted for balance to compensate for the lost portion of the wing, and on we flew.

Before long our group reached the IP (initial point), and we made our turn to begin the bomb run. Once the 45-degree turn had been completed, we were committed and flew a straight line to the target. These were the days of "pattern bombing," with the lead plane carrying the bomb sight and all of the other planes following his lead to the target. Should disaster befall the lead plane, either one of his wingmen could take the lead, as they knew the target also. All planes watched the lead plane anxiously for the bomb bay doors to open, then followed suit.

Everything seemed to be going well until our bombardier threw the switch for the bomb bay doors and called over the intercom, "Bomb bay doors open!" but the doors didn't open!

Since the radio operator sits right near the bomb bay, he could easily see this and immediately came back with, "Radio room to bombardier, bomb bay doors still closed!"

So the bombardier tried a couple more times, but the doors wouldn't open. Deciding they were stuck, the bombardier called over the intercom, "Alright, I'll drop the bombs right through the doors then!" With that, he unloaded the bay and yelled, "Bombs away!" as the bombs knocked the doors open and headed earthward.

But the radio operator came in again, "No! Lieutenant, there is a cluster of bombs stuck in the bomb bay!" So the radio operator and the engineer, braving the bitter 55 degrees below zero temperature and wind blowing in the bomb bay, tried to "kick" them out, but to no avail. Finally, the bombardier came back and somehow got them loose, and away they went. Had they stayed jammed in the bomb bay, I didn't see any way we could have landed safely.

Now a new problem arose. The bomb bay doors wouldn't close, nor would they crank up by hand either. Nothing could be done at this point except to stay with the group and head for home. We made it back to our base at Bassingbourn but as we approached the runway, disaster seemed imminent. The hydraulics on the left side, where the "short" wing was, were gone and very little pressure was left on the right side to bring the landing gear down, but gravity did help. Landing was another story, however, since the pressure was so weak the control surfaces barely responded, which meant we didn't have any flaps for braking. Fighting the controls, the pilot, with the copilot's help, poured the power on engines #1 and #2, to hold that side up where the wing was "short" from the midair collision. The right side, being normal, was heavier and tended to dip down. Should that wing dip upon landing and strike the runway, we would surely cartwheel into a disastrous crash. Skillfully, Lt. Guinn handled the problem, using only the engine power to control the ship, and brought us in safely. But it was like landing on ice.

Plus there was the problem of the open bomb bay doors. The tail had to be kept a little higher to keep the bomb bay doors from scraping the runway too soon. If they did, control could be lost, with unknown results. On the other hand, a

"079" made a surprisingly smooth landing at the home base in England following a midair collision with another B-17 over Germany. "079" was taxied up to the hangar and crew members scrambled out on the chewed-up wing to inspect the damage. On the wing, left to right, 2nd Lt. Robert J. Hornbeck, navigator, of Chicago, Ill; 2nd Lt. Charles A. Guinn, pilot, of Phoenix, Arizona; 2nd Lt. Sidney Edelstein, bombardier from Brooklyn, N.Y.; and 2nd Lt. Kenneth W. Fallek, co-pilot of Greeley, Colorado. Other members of the "Forts" crew looking up at the wing, include, left to right (wearing Mae West jacket) S/Sgt. Harold E. Wingate, engineer and top turret gunner, from Baltimore, Maryland; Sgt. Wm. E. Rassmussen, ball turret gunner, of Cedar, Michigan; and S/Sgt. Bert A. Stieler, radio operator and gunner, of Albany, N.Y.

Other members of the crew not shown are: Sgt. Charles W. Dyer, engineer and left waist gunner, from Spencer, Indiana; Sgt. John Hinda, right waist gunner and armorer of Pittsburgh, Pa.; and Sgt. Gerald E. McDowell, tail gunner and armorer, of Merion, Pa. and also this book's author.

(Remaining five men on the ground are not members of the crew and are not identified.)

"belly" landing would be worse. Then there is always a chance of fire, yet with all the crash landings that occurred from battle-damaged planes returning, I never knew of one to catch fire. There may have been some, but I never saw any.

Bert, our radio operator, had notified the base of our dilemma and as we made the approach, I noticed fire trucks and an ambulance running alongside of us as we touched down— just in case, I guess. Fortunately for us, the good Lord was on our side once again, and although we had a rough landing, we did manage to stay on the runway due to a good pilot. He also kept the plane up on its landing gear until we gradually came to a stop, even though it did take a lot of the runway. The bomb bay doors were badly bent and beat up from scraping the runway as we came in. A truck was there and took all of us back to headquarters for interrogation of the mission. Needless to say, we lost "079," a nice new ship!

So on November 29 we were given a replacement ship that had just been repaired and was now ready to go again. Her name was *Hell's Belle*—A/C #23060—sister ship to the famous *Memphis Belle*. When we walked out to the line to look her over, I could sense her feel of battles past as I circled around her, then stopped near the nose to gaze wonderingly at thirty some mission markings under the pilot's window. I have no idea what became of the crew who flew this airplane previously. Although I do have a photo of a crew posing in front of the plane and the name "Hell's Belle" is easily visible, the crew is unknown to everyone I have asked.

In any case, *Hell's Belle* had just been assigned to the 401st Squadron from the 385th Group just four days before. It seems that a previous crew had put three missions on her, and then apparently they were assigned elsewhere. I could hardly believe that this plane had gotten through those missions, with losses being what they were at that time. Most vividly, I remember to this day the sixteen bullethole patches all around the tailgun position, on the very last section of the tail. Being scattered as they were seemed to indicate that they were a result of several missions. Since the tail gunner sat right between those patches, I wondered how many gunners had been hit, and would I be next?

It was now the twenty-ninth of November and we were made operational for a mission that once again I can't remember, but records show that we aborted for some reason. The following day we were operational again, with another abort. This was November 30.

I should add here that "aborted" and "turn back" missions can be just as disastrous as a completed mission. On the way to the target in those days, your plane could very well be shot down by flak or fighters. I know of some cases in which this happened, especially with flak.

Our next mission would be our eighth and little did any of us know, *our last!* But in this "game" you must take them as they come, one at a time, and pray each time you go out that things will go well and that the good Lord is by your side. We had just lost one waist gunner, John Hinda; frostbite on one ear grounded him and I felt bad about this, as he was my very close friend all through training and the missions we had flown so far. So we now had a replacement waist gunner. Somehow things seemed different to me from then on, for we had now broken up the original crew and it just wasn't the same without my friend John. Even after all these years, I often think about him and wonder how things went for him afterward.

I was told while in Stalag 17-B by a "new" POW that John had stood guard over my locker, even at gunpoint, so no one could touch my things in the locker until he was sure I was not going to return.

Unfortunately only the completed missions were counted towards our twenty-five mission tour. We were required to reach the target, bomb it, and return to get credit for a completed mission. "Scrubbed missions," "turn backs," and "aborted" missions did not count in spite of the danger of flak and fighters encountered during these missions. However, after twenty missions, if you could get that far, each crew was permitted to select the last five missions out of what came along. Naturally the more missions you passed by, the longer you would remain on combat status until twenty-five missions were completed.

In 1943 during the heavy air battles over Europe, rarely did a B-17 return that the tail gunner had not engaged his guns in the air battle that ensued. Tail gunners inflicted the most devastating fire on enemy planes coming in from the rear as it was the most important defensive point on the Fortress during these attacks and one that enemy planes vigorously tried to eliminate first as they came in with guns blazing.

Yet conversely, by the winter of 1944 the Allies controlled the skies and with ample fighter escort to accompany the B-17s, the majority of Fortress gunners never once fired their guns at the enemy!

Chapter Three

The next day was our fateful day: December 1, 1943. As near as I can remember, we were awakened about 3:30 A.M. by Stewart, the bay chief. Chow time was from then until 4:30 A.M., and then came the briefing until 5:00 A.M.. After this, we made such preparations as getting into our flying gear, giving our guns a final once-over, and checking everything essential for the flight until station time at 5:50 A.M. From this point on, it was always a race against time to get those twin ".50s" in the tail of the ship and have my flak vest on—when they were available—all by takeoff time! Believe it or not, at that time flak vests had only been out about six months and there just were not enough to go around. In fact, our 91st Group was the first to test them (March 1, 1943). So, for the moment, it was a first come, first served basis, and this time I didn't get one!

Our primary target originally was the steelworks at Solingen and either Duren or Bonn was our secondary target, also in Germany. However, for some reason the primary target had been suddenly changed to Leverkusen, a large industrial city near Cologne, and we would be going in at 26,700 feet altitude. The change of target had to have come about as a result of a coded message received by the lead plane somewhere on our way to the original target. So, as always, we all followed the lead plane to the target.

For some reason, every squadron put seven planes in the air this day, instead of the usual six. I think it was because of the new offensive named "Operation Stitch," and that meant "maximum effort," anything with wings was going up every day until further notice. I remember the interrogation officer who briefed us on this mission, saying how important this target was to the German war effort and how they would do their utmost to keep us from reaching it and to expect plenty of resistance in the form of their "best!" "Best," to us, meant the "Abbeyville Boys," also known as the "Flying Circus" or "Goering's Own." These were the best pilots in the Luftwaffe. In addition, latest G-2 intelligence reports now showed about *70,000* flak batteries up and down the entire Ruhr Valley. I can still hear that G-2 officer saying, "Now I didn't say 7,000, I said *70,000!*" There would be no way, as in the past, to go around either end of the Ruhr to avoid all this flak. We would just have to go through it as fuel consumption would be too great, so would the risk of exposure to fighters and more flak, for too long a time.

He also added that there had been some reports recently of our airmen being strafed by Luftwaffe fighters while they hung helpless in their chutes. These incidents were unusual and believed to be the act of some bitter Luftwaffe pilots who had just yesterday lost a friend in aerial combat with the Flying Fortresses, or their town or city had been bombed the day before. Therefore, G-2 advised when bailing out over enemy territory to drop at least 20,000 feet before pulling the rip cord. Take a few deep breaths of oxygen before jumping, then hold your breath as long as possible. In a short time, you will have to breathe and the thin air will cause you to pass out. But you should regain consciousness around 10,000 feet, with ample time to open your chute. I remember some crewman calling out in back of me, "Suppose you don't regain consciousness, then what?"

His answer was, "Then you don't have anything to worry about!"

The last comment G-2 made was, "As of this moment, you will no longer use evasive action to avoid flak bursts because it is now so heavy with all the additional batteries of guns, you may zig when you should have zagged, thus flying right into it!" Fortunately, there was no need to fly the length of the Ruhr—just crossing it would be treacherous enough. Now for the mission.

Our pilot, Lt. Guinn, came back to the tail of the ship where I was putting the gun barrels and bolt sections into the gun receivers and, virtually yelling over the roar of all of the engines being warmed up on various Fortresses, asked me if I was all set. When I said I was, he then wanted to know where my flak vest was. I explained that by the time I got dressed and went over to the hut to get one, they were all gone. He quickly removed his and placed it on me without another word. Even though it was much shorter and lighter and meant for pilots and the like, it was still better than nothing. Those used by gunners are much heavier and longer like an apron, and about halfway above the knee. Even though I tried to tell him he had better keep it as it sounded like this mission was going to be a rough one and he would no doubt need it himself, he would not hear of it. Giving me a side glance and a smile, he turned and quickly headed for the flight deck.

I was not only impressed by him giving up his vest, but he suddenly made me feel the importance of being able to protect the ship's tail during combat, and that vest could make a difference between a live tail gunner and a wounded or dead one! The tailgun position has long been recognized as the most dangerous on the airplane. However, I must admit that I never knew it at that time. The other positions were important also, but a B-17 losing its tail gunner was in serious trouble and easy prey for the Luftwaffe once they discovered it. Riding the tail of a plane in this predicament, they could quickly shoot it to pieces, probably costing the lives of ten good men and the airplane. None of the other guns on board were capable of swinging far enough to cover the area of the tailgun position. Without a tail gunner and with an enemy fighter on your tail, your only hope was to "fishtail" back and forth, allowing the waist gunners to fire each time the fighter came into view on the right or left side, before he could slide in back of the tail again. Who knows, you might get lucky.

As I think back, it sure was lonely back in the tail position. To get there, after passing the tail wheel, I got down on my hands and knees and crawled some 10–12 feet or more to the tailgun position. I had twin .50s on a pivot mount, twin canisters of .50 caliber ammo, 500 rounds on each side of me. Also, twin oxygen systems in case one was blown away, as they were sometimes. A piece of armor plate about eighteen inches wide and perhaps three-eighths of an inch thick was directly in front of my chest and was tapered so I could reach around it to operate the old "fifties." It also swung back in case I had to get to the guns for any malfunctions they may have. I sat on a "bicycle" type seat, kneeling right in back of the armor plate as I viewed the sky through a piece of two and three-eighths inch battle plate glass directly in front of me. This gave a perfect line on the iron grid sight mounted outside. The very thick, crystal clear glass would stop machine gun bullets, even a 20mm cannon shell hitting from a wide angle. So you felt as safe as combat would allow, but isolated from the crew if you should need help for some reason, such as being wounded. The thing that bothered me most was all that ammo in those two canisters—1,000 rounds in all, with the tips facing *in* and me sitting right between them! One piece of flak or gunfire coming through the skin of the plane and hitting a primer would be good-bye for me!

Recovering from my thoughts, I hopped into the tail to my position for a final check. Everything looked okay, so I moved up to the waist of the ship with the rest of the gunners and tensely awaited takeoff. Tail gunners and ball turret gunners didn't stay in their positions during takeoff or landing. While waiting, I plugged my headset into an intercom nearby and listened.

The next thing to come over the intercom was, "Army 060, Army 060, you are clear to taxi to the takeoff position."

"060 Roger," replied our pilot. Next came, "Army 060, Army 060, stand by for takeoff."

Again the reply from the cockpit was, "060 Roger." Now the pilot and copilot, working together, "rev" up the engines, checking out the magnetos and several other things, pouring on the power until those four 1,200-horsepower engines reached takeoff speed. The ship vibrated and strained at the brakes like a wild bull trying to break loose of its shackles. Seconds later, the tower gave us the green light. Lt. Guinn kicked off the brakes and the plane lurched forward with demonlike power, roaring down the runway like a wild stallion, seeming anxious to seek and destroy a target.

Climbing steadily, we were soon with the rest of the planes from our group and formed up with the other groups in our wing heading over the Channel to Germany.

Quite some time before we reached the combat area, our lead plane in the squadron reported over the command wave of the intercom that he was aborting due to oxygen failure. His position in the lead now open, the other pilots looked back and forth at each other as they jockeyed for position to tighten up the formation again, trying to decide whether to take the lead or wait for some other plane to take it. Over the intercom I could hear Lt. Fallek, our copilot, prodding Lt. Guinn, urging him to move up to the lead position. "Go ahead, Chuck, take the lead—he's waiting for you. Come on Chuck, move up and take it!"

But Lt. Guinn saw we couldn't move up safely because of other planes above and around us. It would have been very risky, and a midair collision might have resulted. On the other hand, our copilot was a "hot rock" and would no doubt have used full power to pull out then up into lead position, if given the chance. But we didn't move up since the pilot would not risk it and he is the boss. Unfortunately, in not trying, not only did we lose our chance for the lead, but the other planes moving up crowded us out and back until we ended up in the worst place in the formation, "Purple Heart Corner!" No crew wants this spot in the formation. "Purple Heart Corner," or "Tail-End Charlie," as it was sometimes called, was virtually the last plane, in the last element, of the last squadron of the group. Being low group was bad enough. Without question we became a prime target in that position, so it is easy to see how it got its name. At any rate, we fired a couple short bursts to clear our guns once again, and made ready for battle.

It wasn't long after we crossed the coast of Europe that the flak began. It was very heavy for a long time, and as it has been said many a time, "The flak was so thick you could get out and walk on it!" Suddenly, the flak stopped and we waited anxiously, as we knew this meant that the fighter attack was about to begin. Glancing all around the sky, I noted several fighters off in the distance doing acrobatics for us, hence the name "Flying Circus." At one point there were four Me 109s flying almost wingtip to wingtip right at us, while the two inside planes were doing slow rolls in opposite directions and still holding the formation. Very impressive flying, to say the least. These antics were always done out of range of our guns, of course.

Shortly afterward, the show was over and all hell broke loose. Instantly, it seemed like the sky was full of fighter planes (Me 109s and Fw 190s). As they roared through the formation, guns blazing, that three feet of bright yellow paint on the nose of the plane stood out like a sore thumb, as did the prop spinner on others with its black-and-white colors spinning like a barberpole. The battle began and I was firing my twin 50s at anything that gave me a target, even though they seemed to be some 500 or more yards away. They were still within range of my guns, which had an effective range of 600–800 yards, yet were very destructive at even 1,000 yards. I could also hear the guns firing from other parts of our plane, as well as other Fortresses all around us in the formation. Enemy planes were diving through the formation at top speed doing partial rolls, first left, then right, then left, then right, then left again in a rocking motion as they came at us, making a poor target. As they barreled through the formation they would roll over on their backs, turning their bellies toward us, which were very heavily armored, pouring out a hail of gunfire as they came. Even at best, they became a target for only a brief moment, so shooting them down required all the skill you could muster, plus a lot of luck. Most of the attacks came from 12 o'clock and were concentrated on the low squadron of the low group and the group ahead.

I saw tracers bouncing off these planes in all directions as they bored through the formation, their own guns blazing away and their armor plate deflecting our tracers in all directions, sometimes coming from ten or fifteen guns at a time, yet seldom hitting a vital spot. As the onslaught continued, very few enemy aircraft were hit. Those Luftwaffe pilots who had to bail out were able to get another plane and come up tomorrow to fight again. Many of them had been shot down several times.

To increase our effectiveness, a new system of belting ammo had been brought about. Instead of a rotation of ball (plain), tracer, incendiary, and armor piercing types, we went to just one tracer then four armor piercing. This sequence was repeated throughout the entire belt. With 80 percent of the ammo now armor piercing and only 20 percent tracers for aiming purposes, I felt we gained a big edge. It was bound to make our hits much more effective and give better penetration. Even so, you still had to hit a vital spot to bring them down. Nevertheless, the new ammo program proved to be doing much more damage, I'm sure, and brought down some planes that otherwise would have gotten by with just some repairable battle damage. Now they may go down and crash or even be destroyed in midair. In spite of every effort made, the Luftwaffe at present controlled the skies and it almost seemed that for every Me 109 or Fw 190 shot down, there were three more to take its place. (Of course the tide changed several months later, as we all know now.) Even so, the Luftwaffe never once was able to turn back our bombers or keep them from reaching their target.

Pressing onward toward the target as the battle continued, I didn't have time to think of being scared, only to concentrate on the air war at hand and do my job as a gunner. Like all the other aerial gunners, I was highly trained and lived to destroy German aircraft—dutybound to protect the plane from the enemy so we wouldn't get blown to pieces ourselves, and protect my own ass as well!

Suddenly, without warning I felt a hard jolt and was slammed up against the bulkhead right alongside of me. The plane began to buffet and the vibration was unbelievable as she began to nose over. Then a voice screamed over the intercom, "We're hit! We're hit! We're going down!" Slowly, the big bird began to peel off and head downward rapidly, picking up speed as she went. We had been hit hard by two Me 109s coming up from underneath in a frontal attack. The Luftwaffe had quickly learned through combat that their best point of attack on a Flying Fortress was from the front. (When the model B-17G Fortress was introduced later on, a chin turret had been added, with twin .50 caliber machine guns discouraging the frontal attacks considerably.)

But, here again, being in "Purple Heart Corner," we were an ideal target, as I said before. Twenty mm cannon shells came through the air screen and up through the flight deck, tearing up the pedestal. Machine-gun bullets came up through the floor and the air screen, destroying the instrument panel, and passed right between the arms of the pilot and copilot. Broken glass was flying everywhere, yet amazingly neither of them got a scratch. Our #1 engine had been shot up and had to be feathered and shut down. Also, one of the 20mm shells hit our #2 engine, knocked two blades off of the propeller, and blew up the engine. This explosion flipped us up on the opposite wingtip and put us into a dive.

As we picked up momentum, I stayed at my position listening to the intercom, expecting the large "abandon ship" bell just above my head to ring. The bell never rang but the pilot came on the intercom and said, "If anyone back there wants to bail out, just say so, and we'll try to level off. We can't get out up here!" I knew I could go out the small escape door in back of me just under the stabilizer, falling clear of the plane, regardless of the speed or angle, without the plane being leveled off. But what about the others, and would the wings stay on leveling off at this speed? No call came wanting to bail out as we continued the steep glide, our speed still increasing.

Deciding to get the escape door ready for exit anyway, I crawled back, grabbed the emergency release handle that pulled the hinge pins on the door and yanked hard! Nothing happened! I suddenly felt trapped, like a rat unable to get out. Reaching just above my head, I took hold of a horizontal support, drew back, and with all the force I could muster in such a cramped position, I came forward full force on the door with my foot. It gave no resistance whatsoever, because all that held it in place was the slipstream from our speed. It was not jammed as I had thought. Not expecting this, my forward momentum took the door off and I slid out with it feet first, almost up to my hips—and I didn't have my chute on yet! Having heard flak bursts peppering the bottom of the plane like gravel on a tin roof over and over again during this mission, I had wrapped my chute up in the flak vest. I didn't want to find it full of holes in case I needed it. Even though I should have been wearing that vest, I was more concerned about my chute, which might become my only chance of survival. Giving a terrified quick stare at the terrain about 20,000 feet below, I made a desperate effort to pull myself back in. Even with the slipstream tearing at my body, I somehow made it. To this day, I do not know how. I can only imagine that the shot of adrenalin one gets at a time like this helped me.

Here again, being alone back in the tail, none of the others on the crew knew of this. The tail gunner had a "hot" spot alright, but I still liked it far better than being a ball turret gunner. Many turrets had been shot loose from the airplane due to 20mm cannon fire hitting the support column, cutting the turret loose, and the gunners in those turrets fell to their deaths—trapped inside with no chance of escape. Also, the door on the ball turret could only be opened from the inside when turned so the guns pointed down. Many a gunner trapped inside when the turret was disabled in combat had to remain inside while the plane landed in a shot-up condition, or maybe even crashlanded! With your "rear end" only inches off the ground as the plane came in, it could be an unnerving experience.

A chute will not fit inside the turret with the gunner, even though he is the smallest man on the crew. I rode in the ball turret once, and that was enough for me. To the eye, there is no visible support. Just sky 360 degrees around you as you view everything through a round, very thick piece of protective plate glass between your feet, about sixteen inches or more in diameter. All you can see of the airplane is the bottom of the engine nacelles with the props spinning and the under surfaces of the wings and fuselage as you turn the turret. Flying in the ball turret is truly an awesome feeling, as though you are up

*there alone, just hanging in midair. I'll stick to my "hot box"
position.*

Still in the steep glide, we were now doing about 400 mph
and the earth was coming up fast. We were also a long way
from where we had been hit, and the area below us was overcast. Two Me 109s were right on our tail, following us down.
As they narrowed the distance somewhat, I crouched over my
big .50 calibers once again, grasping their handles, and fin-
gered the triggers anxiously as I pondered over whether or not
to open fire. Carefully, I cut a bead on one of them and waited.
I wanted to avoid drawing fire at any cost as we were already
badly shot up, two engines were gone, and we were going
down. Fearful of jeopardizing all of us and having the ship
blown up in our faces by these two Me 109s, I chose discretion
as the better part of valor and just sat at my guns, tensely waiting to see what they would do. I watched their wings for flashes
of gunfire and at the first sign of any, I would certainly open up
and pour it on, come what may! They were well within range
and a straight-on shot for me—they just don't come any better
than this. One plane I probably would have fired on, but to
open up on two might be a mistake if I didn't get both of them
before one clobbered us. Besides, these were the days of plain
iron grid sights and "kentucky windage," at least for all the gun
positions except the two turrets. They had range-computing
sights. So I sat tight, waiting, with my fingers on the triggers.
Shortly, both planes pulled up, knowing well that we were out
of it. As they broke off, one pilot did a loop around us and
while he was upside down over our plane, saluted, then turned
sharply and flew away.

Meanwhile, our pilot was yelling over the intercom to the
bombardier, "Get rid of the bombs, Sid, get rid of the bombs!"
Several seconds later, "Are we rid of the bombs yet, Sid?"

"I'm gettin' rid of 'em now, Chuck!" he yelled.

The pilot yelled back, "I'll get rid of the goddamned

things!" Reaching down and grasping the emergency release, he yanked on it hard. The bomb bay doors dropped open and out went the bombs in salvo. This handle was for emergency release only, should the bombardier's release fail or he was killed or wounded. I later learned that the pilot took this action to clear the remaining bombs from the ship because the bombardier was using the manual release and toggling them off one at a time, instead of a salvo. Quite sometime later, after we were down, he was heard to say, "I wanted to spread them out so they would do the most damage!" Here we are going down 400 mph, about to be killed, and this guy is playing dive bomber with our Flying Fortress! Thinking back now, I can only imagine with his name being Sidney Edelstein, he sensed what his fate might be once the Nazis got hold of him if we survived our present ordeal, so he wanted to get his "licks" in with the Krauts now!

Wondering what was going on elsewhere at this point, I took off the oxygen mask (not needed now), throat mike, and headphones, then crawled back to the door that led toward the front of the plane and opened it. As I peered forward to the waistgun positions, I was amazed to see everything so calm. The two waist gunners were looking out of their open gun port windows, and one was even leaning on his machine gun with his elbows. There was no question now that we would be crashing in a few minutes, yet the only crew members I can see are just standing by? It was futile to yell: I would never be heard and I was fearful of getting too far away from my position if I crawled forward to them. So I closed the door and went back. I didn't get there any too soon, either. Fortunately I plugged in the headphones first, just in time to hear the pilot say, "—for a crash landing." Easily guessing the part of the message that I had missed, I hastily yanked the headphones and throat mike off again and quickly headed for the waist of the ship to prepare for a crash landing with the rest of the crew, except for the pilot and copilot.

Standard procedure had already been taken. The flaps were down one third, the ball turret guns were pointed down, and the landing gear was down about one third also. The bomb bay doors were down already from the salvo action.

A study had shown that the best chance of survival for the gunners is to get to the middle of the plane as fast as possible. Sit on the floor, facing the rear of the plane, with your back against a bulkhead (wall). Pull your knees up under your chin, wrap your arms tightly around your knees, and bury your face in your arms. We all knew this very well and got right to it. The two pilots were strapped in their seats, and the navigator and bombardier were with the rest of us. By now, our #3 and #4 engines had quit, having been raked heavily by machine-gun fire, severing the oil lines in several places.

Still maintaining our near 400 mph speed, we suddenly broke through the overcast at about 1,500 feet and a large freshly plowed field loomed ahead, just below us. Lt. Guinn yelled, "That's it!", and headed for it. Fortunately for us, all the land is put to use in Germany—no overgrown fields or junk. It was clear of trees, fences, and any other objects that would normally have been found in the fields of other countries, ours included. Seconds were valuable at the speed we were traveling, and the ship had to be leveled off somehow to land. You pray that the wings will stay on as you pull out.

Straining at the steering column, both the pilot and copilot desperately tried to pull the ship out of its dive. I believe they even had their feet up on the panel and put their backs into it, before finally pulling the ship out at barely 200 feet, which was quite questionable at all, since there was barely any hydraulic pressure left for the control surfaces. For the most part, we had been actually gliding without engine power once we broke through the overcast. Of course all of this happened in a matter of several minutes, but it seemed like a very long time.

Coming in like a meteor at over 200 mph, we slammed into a huge pile of sugar beets, ripping off the landing gear, then catapulted into the air again for a few hundred feet before slamming down once again with a tremendous jolt. With our forward momentum unchecked, we roared through a sugar beet field, plowing it up for several hundred feet as we bounced and floundered along, before sliding to a halt in an adjoining plowed field. I felt the tremendous force of the crash all through my body as I was slammed first against the side of the plane, then against the bulkhead, which I had tried to brace against for the crash. Ironically, we were just a few minutes from our target, Leverkusen, as we came to a halt in that field. Our crash site was about three kilometers from the village of Drove. Rass, the ball turret gunner, took a glancing blow in the chest from a flying case of .50 caliber ammo and was slightly hurt, but shook it off in a few minutes and was able to move on his own.

Amazingly, the wings held together like only a B-17 could through all of this except for one small break of the right wing away from the fuselage, and the housing of #4 engine broke away slightly from the same wing. Now, did we have a pilot or did we have a pilot. Crash a plane this way today and you have 267 or more dead people, and probably a big explosion to boot.

Naturally, the props were all bent under. Losing two of the propeller blades on that one engine is what caused the severe vibration I had felt just before we went down. I did not know at the time just what had caused it.

Also, shortly before we were hit, two rockets, looking like fireballs, came at us head-on. Suddenly, someone—the pilot I think—yelled over the intercom, "Rockets!" Using evasive action, we were able to pull up sharply just in time for one to pass under us, then dived sharply as the second one made a near miss, passing just above us. From the tailgun position, I saw the smoke trail as they flashed by. I didn't realize what it was at first, seeing it from the back. They had been fired by Me 110s and Me 210s, twin-engine fighters which stayed back from the ensuing air battle and lobbed their rockets at us from outlying positions, while the Me 109s and Fw 190s were boring through our formation with guns blazing away.

Chapter Four

Once we were on the ground and finally came to a sliding halt, we all jumped up and saw that the plane was smoking some, and we smelled the strong odor of the leaking fuel. I seem to remember the navigator shouting, "Let's get the hell out of here before this goddamned thing blows up!" and with that he ran for the door and turned the handle, but it wouldn't open. He shouted, "It's jammed!"

We immediately began to scatter, looking for another means of escape. Bert, still by the door, pulled the emergency release that removed the door's hinge pins and kicked the door open. Meanwhile, looking for another way out, Charlie Dyer, the left waist gunner, pulled the pin holding his .50 caliber gun in its mount, raised it out and up to his chin like a barbell. With one Superman-like lunge forward, he flung that 79-pound machine gun out the waist window some 10–12 feet from the plane.

For a few seconds, I stood there dumbfounded at what I had just seen! But then, Charlie was a strong muscular guy who had always worked hard on the farm back in Spencer, Indiana. With the window opening now clear, he quickly climbed up and jumped to the ground below. I started to follow him out just as Bert got the door open, so I turned and left that way instead. By now all the others were out, and we all gathered to make plans and get away from there quickly before the Germans showed up.

Lt. Guinn was in charge of course, and per regulations,

wanted to destroy the aircraft before leaving. If this was not done, the Germans were known to repair some B-17s and then come up and fly with the formation to learn tactics. On occasions they had even been known to open fire on others in the formation. Suddenly one of our planes would be taking hits and wouldn't be able to tell where they were coming from. Then the Krauts would suddenly break away from the formation, but if discovered, would draw fire themselves.

Knowing all of this, a couple of our crew ran inside our plane to get some thermite bombs. Every plane has them just for this purpose. They are incendiary and burn at about 2,000 degrees Fahrenheit when ignited. Striking the tip down hard on one of the wing tanks, they were laid on their sides. Then we all ran a safe distance from the plane to wait for the hot metal to ooze out, melt through the skin of the wing, hitting the gas tank and—BOOM! We waited for a few minutes but nothing happened. Carefully walking toward the ship, we could see that there was no thermite oozing out. For some reason, the bombs would not ignite.

I guess it was around noon or later by now, and with time being of the essence, we had to leave the plane and get out of there. We had no idea just where we were, nor which direction to go in. Little did we know that the Belgian border was not far away. The pilot, copilot, and the engineer stayed with the plane, determined to burn it. Using a flare pistol Guinn shot flares into the spilled oil in the engine cowlings, but to no avail. The flares seemed to hit too hard and bounced off.

There is something I would like to inject at this point to emphasize just how perilous combat missions were during the period of 1943 until we gained control of the airspace over Europe. At that time the Eighth Air Force was growing, with more and more B-17s, now in the hundreds. However, so was the Luftwaffe, with hundreds of Me 109s and Fw 190s. This gave the Luftwaffe the firepower to send untold numbers of fighters into battle with our B-17s. We would often be attacked by more than one hundred German fighters. Needless to say, the Luftwaffe took a heavy toll on us. German propaganda newspapers I have read regularly referred to Germany as "The Graveyard of the Four Engine-Bombers" to make their Luftwaffe look superior. But again, they never once kept our Fortresses from reaching their target! A bulletin I received from the CBS Video Library, narrated by Walter Cronkite, offering combat tapes to the public, says it all: "No form of combat in World War II was more deadly or harrowing than that endured by Allied bomber crews in Europe!" And the most dangerous position on the airplane?—tail gunner! Now they tell me!

Our tour of duty was for twenty-five missions, but the odds of ever making it seemed impossible. I well remember being told one day that a record kept at our group headquarters at Bassingbourn of the casualty rate showed then that for every one hundred men that flew over the Channel into combat, ninety-eight were killed, one was shot down and taken prisoner, and one man completed twenty-five missions! Which meant to me that by the time one man completed twenty-five missions, the lives of ninety-eight others had been lost and one man had become a POW! Hardly a record that offered any encouragement, to say the least. But then, too, the 91st Group was an early arrival in England and became a good "spit and polish" outfit, well-seasoned in combat, and took untold punishment and had extremely heavy losses for their efforts.

Such was the day of the Schweinfurt raid, for instance.

The staffs of both the 1st and 4th Bombardment Wings had chosen the 91st, because of experience, to lead the Schweinfurt raid long before Bomber Command gave the formal order.

On August 17, 1943, the wing of 230 B-17s set out for Schweinfurt with the 91st Bomb Group in the lead.

Just past the small town of Eupen, Belgium, the wing was suddenly attacked by over two hundred German fighters in a relentless onslaught. Using a frontal attack, they swept across the formation in waves of 10–15 fighters abreast, keeping this up all the way to the turning point at the Rhine River.

The total loss of B-17s at Schweinfurt was thirty-six planes, with the 91st Group losing ten of its twenty-four planes (nearly forty-two percent), with thirty-six men killed out of the ten crews lost. Yet the 91st had the best bombing score overall. The raid on Regensburg, Germany, took place the same day with other groups participating and losing twenty-four planes, bringing the day's total losses of B-17 Fortresses to a staggering sixty, *with ten or more written off due to heavy battle damage. It is estimated that the Luftwaffe's losses at Schweinfurt were 277 planes. Fortunately for us, we arrived at Nutts Corner, Ireland, the day after the Schweinfurt raid and at Bassingbourn about two weeks later, as best as I can remember. I was grateful for that since what followed was bad enough.*

Meanwhile, getting back to the crash site, two of the crew were ill from lack of oxygen. I guess their masks were off too soon preparing for the crash or it was caused by battle damage when we were hit, I'm not sure. Guinn, Fallek, and Wingate were still trying to burn the plane, in spite of the danger in remaining there. The rest of us were told to split up and leave while we could. Before we could, however, we saw two workers from a nearby field running toward us, yelling, "Us friend Polski!" They were Polish slave laborers and believed they were going to be freed. Excitedly, they tried to kiss and hug some of us and shake our hands. We anxiously wanted to get away from there, and they only made it more difficult. We pondered momentarily about whom was "buddying up" with whom when Bert suddenly said, "Come on, Mac, let's go!" So I joined him and we started out briskly in an eastwardly direction, as some of the others headed for a gully nearby that offered some cover. As we left the site, the Polish workers, having gone through the plane, came out with gloves, hats, etc., then disappeared.

I had only stayed around the plane a short time watching what happened before Bert and I left. I glanced over my shoulder as we ran from the plane and saw a flare hit an engine, again to no avail.

As either Guinn or Fallek attempted another try with the flare pistol a German soldier, having arrived, pointed his weapon threateningly and made them put up their hands.

Then the soldier disarmed them, took them into custody and shortly afterwards led them away. Before long, the Germans had a couple of guards stationed around the plane, day and night.

Not long after this, a crew of men arrived and began to dismantle the airplane. It was taken apart in sections in about four days, loaded on a large truck and hauled away.

Many years later, I learned from a German report translated into English that a German eyewitness by the name of John Richter had seen us come down and came to the crash site to watch and take pictures, which was strictly forbidden!

It seems that he saw our vapor trails at high altitude as the formation flew over, headed for Leverkusen. Upon our return a few hours later, he stood outside watching and wondering if we had bombed the ball bearing factories of Fitchel and Sachs, which were very important to the German war effort.

The formation was not flying as high coming back, but as Richter stood watching he immediately noticed our plane flying by itself and much lower than the rest, knowing that we were a straggler. As we continued to lose altitude, he saw that both engines on the left wing were dead and shot to pieces. There was no doubt in his mind that we were going to hit the ground shortly. During our descent, we passed within three-

Down In Germany- Eye Witness Report

When an American B-17 crash landed in Germany after a bombing raid, how did the German civilian populace react? How did they feel? What did they do? An eyewitness account by a German who not only saw the 91st plane Hell's Belle, LLG 42-3060, come down but took pictures at the scene, gives us the impression that the reaction was mostly one of curiousity, and to some degree sympathy, at least in 1943. The story comes to The Ragged Irregular from a German architect, Johann Richter, who saw the plane crash near his small village of Drove, near Duren and Aachen.

His finding the 91st Memorial Association is an interesting story in itself. Woodrow B. Hood II, of Long Beach, Cal., the son of a career Air Force father, in turn joined the Air Force himself as soon as he was old enough in 1966. During his service he married a German girl, Richter's daughter. In looking through his father-in-law's photo album (Richter has been an avid photographer since youth) he found pictures of the downed American plane. Study indicated that the plane might be a 91st aircraft and he contacted the R/I, which was able to positively identify it as one belonging to the 401st squadron, with Edward E. Pinkowski as the crew chief, Matt Pettera as assistant crew chief, assigned to Lt. Gwinn as pilot, and lost after six missions.

The date of the event is recalled by Richter as being in December of '43 or '44, but after such a long time he is not sure. Our records do not give any hint, but since Hell's Belle is a B-17F in olive drab '43 seems most probable. If any members can clear up this point or has additional information please pass the information on to the editor.

Here is Richter's story:

I first saw the flight of Fortresses flying at a very high altitude over my little village of Drove about 10 a.m., going in a southeasterly direction. In about two hours the planes came back, this time flying much lower. One of them was flying very low, with both engines on the left stopped and the propellors not rotating.

A few miles futher on the plane made a crash landing in a farm field. "It was a very skillful landing, uphill on a small hill, just beside a little valley. As the plane was making its long landing descent the plane passed within 300 yards of a German troop concentration training in nearby woods. The landing gear was knocked off when they struck a huge pile of sugar beets," Richter recalls, "but the belly landing was smooth, without much damage to the craft."

Several crew members—four or five—immediately jumped out and headed for a nearby forest; the others stayed around the plane for awhile.

Richter was the first person on the scene, then other curious persons came running to see the downed plane. Though none of the crowd could speak English they concluded that the crew thought they were down in Belgium. The Belgium border is close to the area of the crash. Two Polish prisoners working in a nearby field became very excited, believing that the Americans had arrived to liberate them.

The pilot tried to keep the civilians away from the plane as he sought to set it afire with shots from his flare pistol into the engines, but the flares did not ignite the Fortress.

(continued on page 5)

Curious housewives and children examine Hell's Belle as she rests in the German field near Boich.

At last a German soldier, on leave from the Russian front, arrived at the scene and put the pilot and several crew members under arrest. They were taken to the mayor's house in nearby Boich. The mayor, Karl Nolden, was very much an anti-nazi, and he and his wife fed the captured crewmen and tried to assure them that they would be well treated. Richter's uncle, the village priest and the only English-speaking resident of Boiche, also assured them that there were no SS men in the area and that they had nothing to fear.

Later, two civilian police came by and took the 91st-ers away.

It was reported that some crew members were later captured in nearby Mausauel forest.

Within four days the German army had dismantled Hell's Belle and taken the ship away.

hundred yards of where there was a concentration of German troops training in a wooded area, but apparently they never spotted us.

Through the fields Bert and I went, up one knoll and down the next, moving along briskly. We hadn't gone more than about two or three miles when we ran smack into a few of the home guard, as Bert called them. The one who seemed to be the leader confronted us as the others continued on toward our plane. Bert spoke fluent German, which I didn't know at the time. Watching us carefully, their leader patted our sides, looking for weapons, while making some effort to detain us. Bert never let on that he understood what was being said, but only mentioned that this guy wanted to turn us in. Seconds later, he said something about getting away from there, and with that, we turned away and started through a plowed field in a slow run.

The German stayed on the road alongside the field, keeping pace with us as we ran, yelling as loudly as he could, no doubt to attract others, and waving one arm in a threatening manner. Just what he was yelling I never knew, except that it could not have been good, judging by his raving. If he managed to attract others we could be in real trouble, should they catch us. It was a well-known fact that if you were caught by civilians, they would hang you right on the spot from the nearest tree. G-2 Intelligence had several reports of such incidents on file, and they were quick to remind us of this during briefing. Our only chance of survival if captured was with the military, according to G-2.

I was worried about this Kraut following us and yelling like he was. I said to Bert, "We better grab this guy and knock the shit out him, or we will never get away."

"Why beat up an old man?" he asked. "We can outrun him!"

Well, maybe so, but I also kept watching his other hand, still in his pocket, wondering if he had a gun. We tried running a little faster, and the Kraut started to fall behind. As he did, Bert said, "When we get to the top of this hill, we'll make a run for it." Seconds later we were at the top and he said, "Okay, take off!" I kept watching the Kraut as Bert went into a full run, and when the Kraut's hand finally came out of his jacket empty, I turned on the speed to catch Bert. Away we went, through this plowed field like we were going for the "440" record, leaving our pursuer far behind. After about 150 yards or so, my feet and legs began to feel like lead from running through that freshly plowed field in those fleece-lined flying boots with the electric heated boots inside.

As we came down one grade approaching a dirt road, three more people, dressed like farmers, showed up out of nowhere: a man, woman, and a young person. Promptly they began yelling their fool heads off as they ran down a dirt road, passing by us and following the road's turn, which appeared to head toward a small village in the distance. I soon fell well behind Bert, who was a former track star, although I was able to keep him in sight.

Heading down a small bank and on to some railroad tracks, I was able to go faster, but I just couldn't keep up with Bert. He was well ahead of me when a shot rang out and whistled over my head. Bert told me later that when he heard that shot, his first thought was, *Uh-oh, there goes Mac!* A couple of minutes or so later, Bert slowed down and I caught up with him, and we headed for a wooded area, hoping to hole up while the search was on. Besides, the sleet was heavy now.

There was very little brush of any kind to hide in except for a large growth of some briar bushes just at the edge of the woods, near a clearing. Lying on our bellies, we wiggled deep into them to rest and decide what to do. I must have dozed off and so did Bert, for how long I don't know. Suddenly I felt him poking me and whispering, "Don't move, somebody is coming!" Slowly looking up, just in front of us I saw hunting pants, high black boots, and a rifle barrel.

Bert said softly, "They're looking for us!" Whoever it was passed directly in front of us, not more than six feet away, I would guess. There were three civilians armed with rifles, but they could not see us for the thicket, and all the briars and thorns kept the one nearest to us from walking through it. The nearest one also seemed to just stand for a bit, as though looking and wondering about the thicket we were in, then moved on. He had two dogs with him, but for some reason they never picked up our scent.

As they slowly left the area, Bert and I sat up, opened our escape kits, and discussed our almost daily instructions on what to do if shot down. Turning toward me, Bert asked, "How does my face look; do you think I should look for a doctor or should I try to go on?" As I looked at him, I could see that his one cheek was split open about three inches, badly discolored and oozing. His face was swollen over to one ear, and his eye on that side was nearly closed. He said that this had come from a faulty oxygen mask. No doubt about it, he had a severe case of frostbite and without immediate attention, it would surely become infected and gangrene might set in. I could see in his eyes that he was in pain, even though the split area was numb. He feared infection, I'm sure.

His asking me if he needed a doctor really put me on the spot. As a team, we might have had a chance to escape. Alone, I might be free for a day or so, but too many things were against me. I couldn't speak the language, and even so who would be safe to talk to, or trust? The underground, G-2 found out, was now infiltrated with Gestapo at the other end of the line and just let anyone come through to the end, then grabbed them. There was also the matter of food. Being unable to speak German, stealing food would be the only way and that would be very difficult and quite risky, to say the least. The money from the escape kit would not help if you couldn't talk to someone—this wasn't the movies; this was real! Besides all of this it was December 1, some snow on the ground, and the nights were cold.

I couldn't lie to Bert either just to try to save my own skin by coaxing him to go on. So I told him flat out that his face looked pretty bad and he ought to have a doctor. So he handed me his escape kit with everything in it and told me to go on alone, but he was going down to the village to find a doctor. Making a quick decision and not wanting to leave him alone, I decided if we stayed together things might just turn out a little better, but I didn't know. I also realized that by going down to the village with Bert I would be taking a chance on my life if this did not turn out well. So we wormed our way out of the thicket on our bellies, got up, and headed down the hillside toward the village. Approaching a small railroad station with a sign on it reading "Unter Mauback," we didn't see a soul anywhere so we began calling out, then I finally whistled like you would call a taxi.

It took a while, but suddenly a man came out of the door of the station, dressed like any stationmaster. He took one look at us, got very excited, and began yelling something as he headed back into the station. He came right out again, wearing a bright red cap in place of the dark blue one from a minute ago. He hurried toward us with a gun in his hand. I guess the red cap now made him the "Police," or something. Cautiously, and at a safe distance from us, he stopped and asked something repeatedly. Bert said, "I think he wants to know if we have a gun."

"Pistole? Pistole?" the German kept saying. At that time I didn't know a single word of German beyond "sauerkraut," but eighteen months in Stalag 17-B changed that.

Finally Bert said, "Nein!" (no!), and the man came forward and patted our sides to be sure. He kept motioning for us to keep our hands up, which we did, and Bert kept saying to him loudly, "Kamerad!, Kamerad!" (friend). By now, there were about three other Krauts around us with guns. After having frisked us for weapons the stationmaster led us up the road to a part house, part office with a sign on it reading "Burgermeister" (Mayor).

Once inside, we were confronted by the chief of police. The Kraut with the red cap exchanged a few words with him, then left. We were seated on a sofa in the office as two armed guards stood nearby. The police chief was in a military uniform of some sort, complete right down to the steel helmet, and was obviously all "spit and polish." To impress us, he walked back and forth the length of the room, hands clasped at his back, ranting and raving in the usual German fashion, while occasionally glancing in our direction as he spoke. He stopped now and then and shook a finger at us as he shouted in a threatening manner. When I asked Bert if he knew what the Kraut was saying, Bert said, "He says if we don't tell him where the rest of the crew is he can take us out and have us shot right now, do we realize that? What do you want to do?"

"How do you know that?," I asked, "Do you mean you can understand him?"

Bert looked at the floor and said softly, "Yes."

Well, you could have knocked me out with a soft hat when I heard that. Then, as Bert speaking in German asked for food before we would talk and began to "spiel" off in German, the chief's eyes widened and he was as surprised as I was, maybe more, because of how "clean" Bert's German was—no accent! Now trouble really started. The Krauts wanted to know why a "pure" German would leave the Fatherland and then come back to bomb and kill his own kind. Bert tried in vain to explain that he had not "come back" to Germany. He was an American citizen. The chief would not accept this explanation, so the argument continued for a while. Suddenly I remembered what the G-2 officer told us back at Bassingbourn about the German military: "They will threaten you to the point of execution but will not carry out their threat." Counting on this G-2 officer to know what he was talking about, I said to Bert, "The hell with him, don't tell him anything."

With that, Bert told him that we had all split up and didn't know where any of the others went. Our apparent defiance made the chief really take a fit! So the pacing and yelling started again.

Along about this time an elderly lady, probably his wife, quietly came in with a dish that had a little something to eat on it, cookies as I recall. I felt something bumping my elbow and as I turned I saw this plate being pushed at me. She offered some to each of us, then quickly left the room without a word. It never occurred to me then but now when I think back, I'd bet my silver wings that she was thinking of a grandson she had in the service somewhere or even a son, praying that they might be given some consideration under similar circumstances.

Now, talk about coincidence. Recently I received several pages of copy relating to our shot-down plane crashing in Germany and the surrounding circumstances at the time, as told by eyewitnesses. These four pages of copy became a matter of record in December 1943 in Germany, and now in 1989 while writing this manuscript, I stated what I thought Frau Nolden (actually the mayor's wife, not the police chief's) must have been thinking forty-six years earlier as she gave us food. Ironic as it may seem, my comment about Frau Nolden was written in my manuscript months before I ever received the four pages of printout! This printout became available to me through our 91st Bomb Group historian. In the translation from German to English, I took particular note of a couple of sentences which referred to Bert and I being offered "snacks" by the mayor's wife, as I mentioned in the previous paragraph. Now from the printout record, I quote: "Frau Nolden felt sorry for these young boys. Her son was a soldier on the front line. She hoped someone would treat him as well!" I was overcome by this co-incidence, to say the least, in finding my thoughts to be exactly the same as hers were then! My only error here was that being only twenty years old myself, I misjudged Frau Nolden's age then, thinking she may have had a grandson in the army, rather than just a son.

Eventually, the chief of police had vented his spleen. Marching briskly to the telephone, he made a call which certainly seemed to be about us, the way he frequently turned and glared at us as he talked. Sure enough, sometime later two Luftwaffe men in full uniform arrived and escorted us to a racy-looking sedan, and off we went.

Chapter Five

It was dark by now and with wartime blackouts everywhere, the headlights on the car were just the usual amber slits to drive by. The car was very plush inside. Describing it later to someone from Europe, I was told that it was no doubt a Horch-Wanderer, which was much preferred by the German military's lower-ranking officers. This car, I recently learned, was the forerunner of today's Audi. We seemed to be darting through all kinds of narrow streets and sharp corners in each village we went through, at a speed that had me on the edge of the seat. After all, how could the driver see well with only those two slits of light in front? I decided that he had to be familiar with this area to go zipping through these streets as briskly as he was, although with it being pitch-black those headlights seemed brighter, I guess.

Soon we slowed down to a crawl, and the driver turned off to the right between two big stone pillars at the entrance of what looked like an old bastille surrounded by a very high iron fence. This much I could see in the moonlight. Once inside I seem to remember they took Bert toward another room in the back to look at his face as he kept saying to them in German, "Let me see a doctor, I want to see a doctor!" I was taken upstairs and led down a long, wide hall with cell-like rooms on each side the full length of the hall. The walls on both sides were of solid wood planks about nine or ten feet high and right up to the ceiling. Each cell had a heavy wooden door about 12–14 inches thick with beveled sides like a bank vault door.

I could not see in the cells from the hall. However, each door did have a large corkshaped plug in it, which the guard could swing out to check on the prisoner. All in all, the general construction was quite old, it was plain to see. Suddenly we stopped, the big door was swung open, and I was pushed inside. The sound of that big door as it slammed shut with a "thud" had an awfully final sound to it. I don't know where they went with Bert, but I guessed that they had put him in a cell, too. The cell I was in was about eight by ten feet with a cot on one side and a barred window at the back. The glass was rippled, which kept me from seeing out, but it did allow the light to come in. Sitting down on the cot and wondering what was next, I began thinking of the day's events. The last thing I ever expected was to be shot down and become a POW! This was the first time I was ever in solitary confinement. I don't even remember how many days I was there.

My main worry in combat was being wounded, losing a leg or arm, or just plain being killed from gunfire from a Me 109 or a Fw 190. I had always prayed to God to let me come back the same as I went or not to come back at all. My prayers were answered. Lying back on the cot, I soon dozed off as the strain of the day caught up with me, and I fell into a sound sleep.

Early the next morning, I awoke suddenly from a dream—I had just shot my way out of this place with a .45 automatic in each hand. As I sat thinking how ridiculous that was, I heard the marching of leather boots coming down the hall. Suddenly they stopped, then there were voices, and they marched away again. All was quiet until I heard what sounded like commands, then two or three bursts from a few "burp" guns. Then all was quiet once again. Instantly I felt that someone had just been executed. Could it have been Bert, I wondered? Not long after this, I heard the boots out in the hall again, this time coming closer and closer to my cell. They stopped, the latch went

71

clunk, and the huge door swung open. Immediately I knew I was next for the firing squad and the gunfire I had heard was the firing squad executing Bert.

Thank God, I was wrong, and my imagination had been running away with me. They had really come to take us elsewhere and as they escorted me downstairs, I saw Bert coming forward from a lower room with his face bandaged. Once outside, we were put in a car and driven to a Luftwaffe base, which as I recall was just outside of Cologne. Here we were taken to a cellar where a guard stood over us, I guess because they didn't have a cell here. As we were being taken in, I saw some Fw 190s warming up and one even taxied near us as he made ready to take off. We no sooner got inside and down in the cellar than the air raid siren went off, which explained the Fw 190s warming up. Minutes later, our B-17s were unloading their bombs and I couldn't believe the tremendous noise and shock waves that rocked the building. Mortar and pieces of whitewash fell all around us from the stone walls, with each blast of those 500-pound bombs. The concussion of the nearby German 88 *antiaircraft* batteries was extremely heavy, too, as they fired on the B-17s passing overhead at high altitude. These guns could reach above 40,000 feet but accuracy dropped off 50 percent every 5,000 feet above 15,000 feet. It was amazing to me that the Germans could continue to take such a pounding day after day from us, then take it all over again every night from the Royal Air Force with their 1,000- and 2,000-pound "block busters," and this went on endlessly day after day.

Soon the bombers passed, and they took us outside to a truck. Apparently we had just stopped here so everyone could get inside out of the air raid. It didn't appear that the airfield took much damage, fortunately for us.

From here we went the rest of the way to Cologne. By now we had to go to the toilet. I guess Bert told the guard, and he said something in German and pointed toward the hedgerow near us. So here we are right in the middle of the city of Cologne, the railroad station on our left, trolley cars coming and going and people bustling around all sides of us, and this guy says just walk up to the hedges and "go"! Well, it wasn't easy, but oddly enough the people didn't seem to even notice us!

On the way to the station, we met other guards with a couple more of our crew, but I can't remember who. One of the other crewmen apparently needed to go to the toilet, so the whole group was taken downstairs in Cologne railroad station. Believe it or not, there was a middle-aged woman there working as attendant in the men's room. Many men were there using the urinals, and she very casually went from one vacant urinal to another, wiping the top of them with little regard for the man using the urinal next to her, nor did he seem to notice her. One man came out of a stall and she quickly walked in and flushed the toilet. As she came out, he handed her a coin and went on his way. As I watched all this while waiting for the others, I thought to myself, *now I've seen everything!*

We were soon in the truck again and headed for Frankfurt. Our truck stopped at a marshaling yard on the edge of the city, and we all were taken into a small POW camp there. It was dark now, and inside it was very dismal and dimly lit. The building seemed very old and held only a small number of prisoners. Most were British. The quarters were rather cramped although I believe there was an outside exercise yard used in the daytime, which was well-wired and well-guarded, of course. After being given a typical POW bit of chow, we sat down on a cot with some of the resident POWs to find out what the place was like. We did not know if this was our camp for the duration, or not. They were quite unhappy of course, and everyone had the same fear and that was an air raid. The marshaling yards here were vital to the German war effort, and I believe there was a much-needed chemical plant nearby.

To protect the plant from bombing, the Nazis built this POW camp in the middle of all of this, knowing that the Allies would not bomb a POW camp, unless by mistake! Also, you can rest assured the Germans knew that the Allies knew the camp was there. One of the prisoners told us everyone was on edge just waiting for the "hit" that they knew would come sooner or later, if they were not taken away from there soon. How right he was! We left a few days later and a new arrival at our next stop said that the camp had been hit a night or so after we left. Certainly the Royal Air Force hit it by mistake, due to their night flying, I would say. Even though the "Pathfinders" accurately mark the target for the bombers, mistakes can be made and somehow one bomb might go astray—proving most unfortunate.

As we made our way into Frankfurt, along the streets the damage was unbelievable. Not one building with a roof or four walls as far as the eye could see, and rubble everywhere up and down both sides of every single street from the crumbled buildings. There were no sidewalks; they were completely covered. My first thought was, *any further air raids would be just turning over all of this destruction,* for there was nothing else to blow up. Some of our guys started to howl and laugh at all of the different blown-up buildings with, "Look at that one, ha, ha!" and "Look at that one over there, ha, ha!" Wisely, Lt. Guinn told everybody to knock it off lest the guards or anyone else become infuriated over our actions for poking fun at their dilemma. Then too, us being "Der Flieger Gangsters," as we were known to them, (The Flying Gangsters), they see us as the cause of all this destruction. Who knows what they might do? Actually the Krauts feared us to a large degree because they honestly believed we were all Chicago gangsters, taken from jail and put in heavy bombers to destroy Germany, thus our name. Make no mistake either of just how the Krauts felt about any American airmen, and I mean *all* the Krauts, even the chil-

74

dren. For example, sometime during our early capture, a number of our crew had been brought together and taken on foot to a particular location momentarily. As we shuffled along a dirt road, with the line of us sort of drawn out, we passed through a very small hamlet. Several people stood along the side of the road and jeered and shook fists at us as we passed by. I took particular note of two or three children, maybe ten or so years old, as they too jeered and yelled loudly at Lt. Edelstein, "Juda! Juda!" meaning "Jew! Jew!" Now this told me that age was not a dividing line and parents and propaganda taught everyone pride in being a Nazi. Their feelings were nationwide. Even yet today I hear, "Oh, but they weren't all like that!" Bullshit! I was there, and a Kraut was a Kraut.

Another of the many incidents that happened near the end of the war was when we had been liberated at Branau, Germany. Branau is the town where Hitler was born, divided by the Inn River, half in Germany, half in Austria. One of the men of the 34th Armored Division told me that as they passed through a small town, an eight-year-old boy stepped out of a doorway and shot an M.P. in the back, killing him. As I said, Krauts were Krauts, any age, any size. Ask any former combat crewman who was a POW. Incidentally, if I seem to sound bitter, it's only because I am!

Following that incident, there was a white flag of surrender flying high on a building, in another town, as the troops cautiously entered. Suddenly a shot rang out, fired by a sniper in a tower. It struck the jeep in which the commanding officer was riding, but fortunately he was not hit.

Then, according to this soldier from the 34th, word was immediately sent ahead as follows: Should even a single shot be fired on the American troops as they entered the next town flying a white flag of surrender, that town would be leveled, killing every person in it.

As our troops rolled into the next town, it too was flying a white flag high on a mast. Every soldier was ready. The big guns on the tanks were turned outboard, pointing at buildings, and men stood ready at the big .50-caliber machine guns on the half-tracks. Every armored vehicle brandished its fire-power, waiting, as they moved forward.

Suddenly a shot rang out from atop one of the high buildings. Instantly, the American force opened fire with everything they had, destroying buildings and shooting every person they saw trying to escape the onslaught. In a short time they had just about leveled the town.

When it was over and all was quiet, the Americans moved on to the next town. Needless to say, from there on, no more shots were fired at them where a white flag flew.

This was that soldier's story, I wasn't there.

Now the truck pulled up to a sort of hexagonal building known to all as "Dulag Luft," an interrogation center! Treatment was exceedingly harsh, with solitary confinement, little food, and threats of violence. I had concealed a tiny compass in the chewing gum in my mouth much earlier and placed it under my tongue, in case there was a chance for escape. There was a strip search and the Krauts took everything but my skin, but they didn't find the compass. They took leather jackets from all flying crew members, which most men wore at the time of their capture. For some reason, I didn't wear mine on this mission. Some were returned after constant protests. Shortly after this, I forgot and bit down on the gum and broke the glass of the compass, so that was the end of that. Dulag Luft was also a prison, with the same type high wooden walls on each side, the same as the other place Bert and I were in except that the hall seemed much wider here. We could not see into the cells here either, just an outline where the door was cut into the wall. The one difference I did notice right away was a white signal arm at the side of the door that the prisoner could pivot up to signal the guard for something.

This was the first time I saw any of the other crew members since we crashed about a week or ten days ago. We were all herded into some sort of an office to wait. As we waited, "Windy," the top turret gunner, looked at me and asked if I knew that I had the button down on the intercom during the heat of the battle with the Luftwaffe the day we were shot down. I told him that I didn't, and asked what he meant. He said, "Well, when the lead was really flying, you were yelling over the intercom, 'Come on, you sons-a-bitches, come on in and get it.' "

I said, "Yeah, and they came in, too, didn't they?"

He instantly replied, "Yeah, and they got it, too, didn't they?"

I suddenly realized he was referring to a Me 109 that had made a pass at us right across the tail from upper left to lower right, coming within about 200 yards of my position. As he came barreling in, I opened fire with my "twin fifties" but couldn't track him for more than two or three seconds as he passed under us. He must have been going about 400 mph, maybe more. I quickly looked out the right side window near my head and saw smoke coming from his engine as he banked left and turned away from our formation, still going down, as I turned back to my guns looking for other enemy planes. At that time, I never knew for sure if I had made a kill or not until "Windy" said what he did. Being in the top turret, he was probably better able to follow the "hit" than I was. *But,* I thought at that time, *how will I ever get the Air Medal for this "kill" when we are POWs in Nazi Germany?* I thought, *If we ever do get home again, the war will be over and too much time will have elapsed for verification and anyway, who will care?*

We never did have a chance to exchange stories with each other about the recent events since we had crashed and just what had happened to each of us. However, Lt. Guinn was quickly aware of the fact that Lt. Sidney Edelstein, our bombardier, was not present. I remember him saying that the last he had seen of "Sid" was when they first arrived at Dulag Luft a couple of days earlier, and one of the SS "Black Shirts" had Sid down on his knees, forcing him to lick the Nazi's boots.

My thoughts were suddenly interrupted as the door swung open and in walked what later turned out to be an interrogation officer. I think he was either a captain or a colonel, but it was much too soon to have learned their rank. With his arrival, we all became silent and just stared. There was a Luftwaffe pilot with him, and would you believe, he had flown one of the two Me 109s that had shot us down!

Using the interrogation officer as interpreter, the fighter pilot and Lt. Guinn, our pilot, exchanged a few words. All that I learned was that the Me 109 pilot was only nineteen years old, but then, weren't we all, or not much more.

After this, we were split up and put in individual cells, unable to see each other or talk with anyone.

My cell was quite small and this time, no window! No one came around, day or night , except a guard with food. The little I did get to eat was generally very poor, consisting of two slices of black bread and jam with ersatz (substitute) coffee in the morning, watery soup at midday, and two slices of black bread at night.

Here was the last time I saw any of the officers till after the war due to the fact that the Nazis sent our pilot, copilot, bombardier, and navigator to Stalag Luft 1 at Barth, Germany, which was on the coast of the Baltic Sea. The rest of us were sent to Stalag 17-B at Krems, Austria.

There was no doubt that the living conditions here at Dulag Luft were expressly designed to lower morale and cause mental depression. Yet most of us successfully withstood the harsh treatment and refused to give any information to the Germans other than name, rank, and serial number. Most of us were full of hate for those bastards anyway.

The days wore on and about the fifth or sixth day, the cell door swung open and a German guard beckoned for me to come out. He then took me to another room down the hall where a uniformed Red Cross soldier greeted me. He had Red Cross insignia on his blouse and spoke very good English, but the German accent was quite noticeable and his choice of words was somewhat amusing at times, as he pretended to be my "friend." It was not difficult to see through his "act"— clearly. He was very solicitous and as friendly as my mother. The Germans obviously felt that after sitting in a small cell for five or six days, unable to see out and not seeing anyone, you would be glad to talk freely to someone—anyone! He kept asking me all kinds of questions about the mission, how many planes there were, what group I was from, etc., etc. I kept saying, "Name, rank, and serial number is all I am required to give you under the terms of the Geneva Convention."

In turn, he kept repeating to me, "Come man, it is known to me."

Finally I said, "If all this information is known to you, why do you keep asking me for the answers?"

After twenty or thirty minutes of this, he signaled for the guard. He realized I was dodging all of his questions, and he gave up trying and had the guard take me back to my cell.

In the cell next to mine I could hear someone yelling, "Get out'a here, you son of a bitch, I'm not telling you anything!" Later I learned there was a Mosquito pilot in that cell and he had been there for forty-some days. It's a wonder he hadn't flipped out by then. The British Mosquito airplane was rather new to the Germans about then, and they surely wanted to learn all they could about it. It was a twin-engine fighter/bomber with plywood wings feathered to an almost "razor" edge. It was very maneuverable and very fast, as the Luftwaffe soon found out. Listening closely from my cell, I could tell by the voice that the Mosquito pilot next door was being questioned by the same "clown" in the Red Cross uniform who had been working on me. Though the Germans couldn't learn anything from him, they still kept trying, day after day!

Sometime later I was taken to a rather large office where a German officer sat behind a desk, sort of studying me as the guard brought me in. He was a colonel, I believe. He politely asked me to sit down, then rose to offer me a cigarette from a small box on his desk. Deciding he was trying to give me some kind of a "dope" cigarette to smoke, I refused. (Maybe I had seen too many spy movies, or something). Even so, I was the enemy in a country that was very suspicious of everybody, even their own kind! Of course, the cigarettes were perfectly normal. Any soldier, in any war, enemy or not, always seems to offer the other soldier a cigarette. This was his way to "break the ice" before starting the interrogation.

Then began the interrogation. First off, he wanted to make it clear that our mission was a complete failure since we dumped our bombs out in an open field somewhere, as did the rest of the planes. He then showed me on a large wall map just where they did land. Bullshit, too! Maybe *we* didn't hit the target because of being shot down, but the other planes sure plastered it.

Next, he wanted to know how many planes were at our base. I told him I did not know, there were too many to count. Then he asked, "What was the number of your airplane?"

I said, "I don't know that either because it is dark when we come out for a mission." (Which it was, getting up at 4:30 A.M.)

He said, "But you must see your airplane sometime in the daylight; you use the same one all of the time, don't you?"

I said, "No, we have hundreds of planes, and we use a different one every day!"

After a few more questions with more indifferent answers

from me, he let out a heavy sigh of disgust. Pursing his lips, he reached down to a desk drawer and pulled out what looked like a classified phone directory. On the front in big bold letters was printed, "*91st Bomb Group*"! Slamming it down on the desk, he said, "Alright, if you won't tell me, I will tell you!" With that, he quickly thumbed through the big book for a moment, then flipped it open on the desk and started to read. He started with the name of my induction center and followed that with every air base where I went for gunnery, flying, tech school, or any other training. He covered every stop I made all over the USA *and,* in 1,2,3 apple-pie order! Each time he named another air base, I slid down further and further in the chair from amazement. Then he even showed me a picture of our headquarters building, which appeared to have been taken right on the apron in front of the building! One would have to admit that this was quite a piece of intelligence work. Now that he had put on his little "show" there wasn't much more to be said, so he had the guard take me back to my cell.

I guess the rest of the crew had similar experiences with their interrogations, but oddly enough, no one ever brought it up for discussion later. The only one I heard about was "Rass," the ball turret gunner. When he came in for interrogation and was offered a cigarette, he said, "Sure!"—and took a handful, and he doesn't even smoke! But this was obviously done to aggravate the officer, you can be sure. He constantly interrupted the interrogator, asking about his medals, like: "What's this one?" or "Hey, this is a nice one, what's it for?" Other things he did riled the officer so much that he finally had Rass taken outside and put under the building, where he spent the night out in the open air—*and it was cold!*

I don't remember what else he did, or if anything else happened the next day. In any case, we were all kept there for ten days in solitary confinement.

Chapter Six

Leaving Dulag Luft, we were put on trucks and taken down to a railroad yard in Frankfurt. From the trucks, we were put in those dinky boxcars, the same as they used to take the Jews to the death camps, and we were packed in the same way, about fifty or so men to a car. Straw was strewn about the floor and there were benches along both sides, which were immediately occupied. The only air and light in the car was that from the sliding door being left open a little, but was well covered by a guard. The car was very cramped and uncomfortable to stand in, with nothing to hold on to as the train rumbled along. Pushing through the crowd, I made my way to the side of the car. Getting down on my knees and moving legs and feet to one side or the other, I wormed my way in under a bench and onto some bunched-up straw. The train rolled along, and the clickety-clack soon made me doze off. Later, I woke up and felt I had to "go." Making my way to the door, I tried to tell the guard with gestures and the proper German word for it, which I had just learned. Sliding the boxcar door open a little more, but not enough that I might jump out, the guard said something in German as he motioned a couple of times for me to "go" out the door. Let me tell you, it's not easy to "pee" clear of yourself out the door of a boxcar rumbling down the tracks at a fair speed. But you just stand up close against the edge of the door toward the rear of the train, and let the air flow on the train do the rest!

Working my way back to where I had been, I once again crawled under a bench and went to sleep. The days rolled by with very little to eat. As I recall, when we did eat, they took us off the train long enough to feed us right alongside the box-cars. They gave us watery soup and maybe a slice of black bread, I don't remember for sure. But it was terrible food. After traveling for seven days, we pulled into the outskirts of a town called Krems, in Austria, which was about forty miles north-west of Vienna. It was just about dark as we climbed off the train here, bound for a POW camp on top of a nearby domelike mountain, a camp known as Stalag 17-B.

As armed guards marched us along the road and up the hill to the camp, the twilight was fading, and darkness had set in as we reached the main gate of the camp. Once inside the gate, we were led into a building which was very dismal inside, with almost no lighting except in a couple of areas, black-out regulations I guess. Here, one by one, we had "mug shots" taken and pasted on a large POW file card along with name, birth date, and serial number. We each got a German dog tag with our POW serial number, to be carried at all times. Even after all these years, I still have mine: it is serial #100478. I think we were searched again and checked over generally and also issued two *thin* blankets, which were referred to by the Kriegies as "table covers" and were just about as thin. The term "Kriegie" was our short for "Kriegsgefangenen" (Prisoner of War).

As I moved up in the line, I came to a German soldier sitting on a stool with a small floodlight near him. On the floor beside him was a pail of liquid with a big stick in it. As I approached, he touched my pants and motioned for me to take them down, as well as my undershorts. As the floodlight shone on my privates, he used the stick from the bucket, which had the last few inches at the end wrapped with burlap, to move "things" around as he closely examined my pubic hair. He said something, then dipped the burlap-covered stick in the bucket, had me spread my legs, then "swabbed" me heavily through my crotch twice and over the pubic hair. I immediately caught the scent of the liquid—it was kerosene! For a time I didn't notice anything except the odor. But as we left the building and

The filing time shown in the date line on telegrams and day letters is STANDARD TIME at point of origin. Time of receipt is STANDARD TIME at point of destination

1943

VPAR85 44 GOVT=WUX WASHINGTON DC DEC 13 1036A

MRS JENNIE MCDOWELL=

:MERION GARDENS MERION=

:THE SECRETARY OF WAR DESIRES ME TO EXPRESS HIS DEEP REGRET
THAT YOUR SON SERGEANT GERALD E MCDOWELL HAS BEEN REPORTED
MISSING IN ACTION SINCE ONE DECEMBER OVER GERMANY PERIOD
IF FURTHER DETAILS OR OTHER IMFORMATION ARE RECEIVED YOU
WILL BE PROMPTLY NOTIFIED PERIOD=

ULIO THE ADJUTANT GENERAL.

walked through the snow headed for our barracks, the kerosene began to burn like fire, making it difficult to walk normally, and kept burning for an hour or two.

Before long we reached our assigned barracks, #18A. We entered the barracks like a herd of buffalo, stomping down the middle about four or five across, everybody seeking a choice bunk. It seemed at first as though every POW on that train was coming down the aisle, there were so many. Rass, Dyer, Wingate, and I took the top portion of a corner bunk. Stieler wasn't far behind the rest of us, but for some reason went through the door to the back half of the barracks for a bunk, but things worked out. It was very cold inside, no heat, and just a few American POWs in about the middle of one side, where they had walled in two or three beds using cardboard from Red Cross parcels to form sort of an office with a doorway. This helped keep out the cold some, I guess, and also turned out to be where our barracks chief and his assistant bunked—self-appointed, no doubt. But then, they were here first, so why not? I don't recall anyone else even wanting the job as the months wore on.

This camp was located on the same longitude as the northern tip of Maine and it was about the middle of December besides, making for a cold combination. Climbing up to the top half of the bunk, which slept four, Dyer and I took one half and Rass and Windy took the other. The bunk was certainly rugged and crudely built, and as I seem to recall, it had two by sixes for legs, with two by eights for the sides and ends. It was made to sleep eight persons, four up top and four below. It had enough wood slats to support the necessary sheets of one-quarter inch plywood to form the bottom for a bed, upon which was what the Germans called a "palliasse." It looked like straw burlap and was stuffed with only enough loose straw to give just a little padding, but was by no means comfortable. It quickly became a haven for fleas, which the camp was loaded with, we soon found out. It also became very hard and lumpy in a short time.

I couldn't remember when we had eaten last, and it was plain to see we wouldn't get anything until morning—maybe! Lighting was poor and many light bulbs were missing and never replaced. We were hardly settled before the lights, poor as they were, went out. So we all wrapped ourselves up in our blankets, keeping our overcoats and caps on, and tried to go to sleep in spite of the cold. I remember lying there shivering until I fell asleep.

That first winter was very miserable for us. We were not used to these conditions, and the barracks were terribly cold and damp without heat. Science tells us each person generates 80 watts of heat, but it took some time before we could notice a difference. Then it was just cold, instead of a "walk-in" refrigerator. Then too, there were Kriegies (POWs) making "brews" all day long in the two little chimney fireplaces, which helped generate some heat. The floor of the barracks, although made of heavy wood planks, was covered with dirt apparently dragged in from outside and must never have been swept. You couldn't even see where the planks joined. The only broom we were given was a bunch of thin two-foot sticks, from some shrub, tied together near one end.

Man from Philadelphia Area Missing

Sergeant Gerald E. McDowell, 20, of Merion Gardens Apartments, Merion, has been missing since a raid over Germany on December 2. An only child, he was a Flying Fortress rear gunner. He was graduated from Sheffield High School in June, 1941. After working several months at the Bendix plant he was inducted in January, 1942. His father is superintendent of the American Railway Express here.

SGT. GERALD E. McDOWELL
Merion
Missing

86

STALAG XVII B

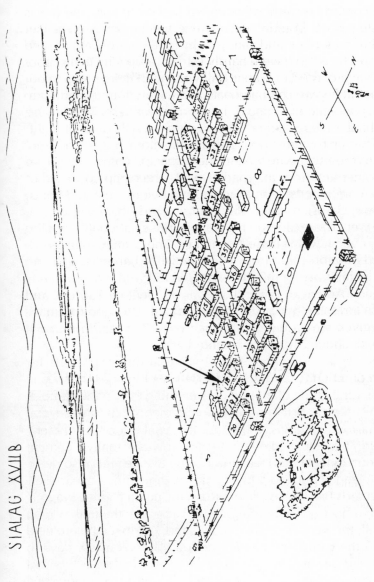

This is a sketch showing only the American compounds (barracks with numbers). A full compliment of POW's, including American airmen, was 30,000 total. 18A (arrow) was where six of our crew, including me, were housed. Original by Ben Phelper

The next morning was our first look at the outside world of Stalag 17-B. Double barbed-wire fences about eight feet high and about ten feet apart, with endless coils of barbed wire in between, completely surrounded the camp with guard towers at each corner and other towers spotted at intervals in between. Each tower had a guard in it twenty-four hours a day with a mounted machine gun and a searchlight. There were also shade-covered street lights to illuminate the area at night.

The entire camp was divided up into a huge "gridiron" pattern by barbed-wire fences to separate the compounds from each other and from the road as well. The camp consisted of twelve compounds, with Americans in five of them and Poles, Russians, Serbs, Slovaks, Italians, and French in the others. There were nearly 30,000 POWs of various nationalities in the camp, over 4,200 of these Americans. The camp was in use as a concentration camp from 1938 until 1940, then French and Poles began flowing in as the first POWs.

Each American compound was 525 feet by 150 feet and held four double barracks (100 feet by 240 feet)and four hundred men were crowded into each one. They had been built to house about 240! Each double barracks was divided by a washroom in the center. There was one outdoor latrine for each compound. Oddly, it was very well-made, when you consider the crude condition of everything else in the camp. It was completely brick: no doors, a cement floor, and several long narrow windows at the top. It was about a fifty "holer," and didn't get cleaned out very often. It was actually a cement pit about 25 feet by 50 feet and maybe twelve feet or so deep. It was cleaned out about twice, maybe three times a year. German guards would have some Russians pull a "honey wagon" in with a big hose and pump it out. Each time the tank wagon was full, the Russians pulled it, by hand, out to the potato field next to the camp and spread the load. It took a few days to empty the pit, and the stench was nauseating for a time. At night you couldn't go to the outside latrine or you would be shot without warning! You had to use the "one holer" outside on the porch area, summer or winter. Should you become ill during the night you go to the porch area and shout to the nearest guard for help, then wait!

A wide dirt road ran down the center of the camp and large gates were along the side at each compound, as well as at the dividing fences where they crossed the road. This "section" method gave the Krauts quick control should a riot break out. They also used one double gate to separate the Americans from all the other nationalities in the camp. We were not required to work under the laws of the Geneva Convention since our rank prohibited it. All other nationalities were made to work. Consequently, we were not permitted through the gate to mix with the others, but a lot of trading went on through the fence, unseen by the Jerries. That's how radios (crystal sets) were obtained. Hundreds of the other nationalities were constantly out of the camp working in salt mines or elsewhere. Now and then a huge group would return just after another group had left.

Each morning around seven thirty or eight o'clock, we were all "whistled" out into the compound for roll call and sometimes for a picture check, too. Frequently, to sort of keep us off balance, they would have two roll calls a day, sometimes three, even four. They would take from one to three hours. An afternoon roll call seemed like it was just for the aggravation. During these formations we were regularly read an order by the sergeant on duty. This order emphasized that, "ANYONE TOUCHING OR CROSSING THE WARNING WIRE WOULD BE FIRED UPON IMMEDIATELY WITHOUT WARNING!"

The "Warning Wire" was a single strand of barbed wire supported by stakes about two feet high. It ran around the entire inside perimeter of the camp, about twenty-five feet from the outer fence, and was clearly marked at intervals.

The next night, at Dyer's suggestion, we opened our two blankets out full and put them together, sleeping under both of

Kgf.-M.-Stammlager XVII B
Teillager der Luftwaffe
Lagerführung

Gneixendorf, June 11th 1944

Warning!

1.) Any P.o.W. touching or crossing warning wire during day-time will be fired upon immediately.

2.) From taps to reveille (to-day from 9⁰⁰ p.m. to 5⁴⁵ a.m.) do not leave barracks except in case of air raid alarm nor use latrine! Use night toilet only at end of barrack!

3.) Any P.o.W. outside barracks at above time will be fired upon without warning. In emergency cases (falling ill etc.) do shout loudly to the nearest guard!

Hauptmann and 1st Lageroffizier

Copy of original Warning! poster placed on the porch area of POW barracks.

them. This way we got some body warmth from each other to help keep warm, but we needed to keep our overcoats and caps on, too.

In the months that followed, the rations were pretty sad in both quality and quantity. The chart I kept shows the sort of food the Germans fed us at Stalag 17-B. It covers February and most of March of 1944. There was no need to continue as it never changed.

The soup was always the same—rutabaga! One dipper per man and lots of little white cabbage worms floating in it! The raisins and the prunes were stewed and plain, one ration per man given out by our "chow man." A small portion of canned salmon or spam and two boiled spuds was considered a meal. Hot water meant just that, HOT WATER!, that's all. Some Kriegies made instant coffee with it, others shaved with it, but most never even got in line for theirs!

The only decent thing we ever got from the Germans was the cooked barley and raisins ration.

There were no rations given for the evening meal on Saturday or Sunday as shown by the dashes on the chart. But they were spruced up a bit when the International Red Cross Committee and Protecting Power were due to visit the camp. This was about every three months. I dare say I never saw them but once in the eighteen months that I was there. When they left, it was back to short rations and crappy food. In January of 1944, our rations were cut in half when the Germans claimed we had adequate food from them along with our Red Cross parcels, but the parcels ran out May 5 when those left were issued *one* to each *five* men, instead of the usual one per man per week! Yet the Red Cross in Switzerland claimed that over 42,000 parcels had been shipped in May to Stalag 17-B. Investigation showed that the parcels were sent out promptly to the POWs and all delays could be blamed on the Germans. There was no doubt in our minds that these bastards were just holding out on us.

Capt. Stephen Kane, a priest, was our only chaplain for all of the denominations, and for some reason, the Krauts watched him closely. He had a wonderful rapport with all the GIs in the camp, regardless of their religion. We had four American doctors and a dentist who had been captured also. I was told that one of the doctors or the chaplain had allowed himself to be captured so he could be with POWs and offer help to them. How admirable!

Each day, a team of two men went to the camp kitchen for a large "tub" of soup. The tub had a lid and a long pole through the top of it so two men could carry it on their shoulders back to the barracks. One time I was helping to carry the chow bucket and it suddenly slopped out over my clean pants. Instinctively I yelled, "You son of a bitch!" To my embarrassment, Father Kane was standing nearby, and as we passed, he pointed to the man helping me and said to me, "What did you call that man a son of a bitch for?", then smiled.

Once the tub of soup reached the barracks, it was rationed out by one of our guys who willingly took on the job of "chow king." He saw to it that everyone got a fair share. More often than not, the big tub was filled with rutabaga soup, which we all hated, mostly because of the little white cabbage worms that were always floating in it. One man was appointed "chow man" for several bunks in a section. When any other chow such as black bread or other rations came, each chow man was called up to the center of the barracks where the barracks chief and the chow king gave each chow man an equal share for his section, which he in turn divided up with the men. Many, many times the black bread was moldy, and if your ration was, that was your tough luck! When you would start to complain to the other guys, someone would always say, "Look what you got that nobody else did!", so you couldn't help but laugh a little. Most Kriegies swore the black bread was loaded with sawdust.

Our diet for breakfast was prunes one day and hot water

the next, alternating every other day. Periodically, we received a ration of what looked a little like raspberry jam but sure didn't taste like it. We called it "Jerry Jam" and all stopped eating it when the word got around as to what the Russians working in the kitchen were "doing" in it! They thought the Germans were eating it, not us. The Krauts knew we had Red Cross parcels and could make instant coffee with the hot water, so that was all we got every other morning.

The Red Cross parcels, depending on just how many the Jerries allowed us to have, were divided up as equally as possible by our men in charge. This came out to about two, sometimes three men to a parcel. When things really got tight, it came down to 5–7 men to a parcel, even though they were really meant for just *1 man* for *1 week's* rations! So you can imagine how little each man got. When we did get the parcels, everyone went through a line where a Jerry guard waited to see you throw at least two or three empty cans in the nearby bin as you passed, or he would not let you get in the line for a Red Cross parcel. Another way to be sure you were not storing cans of food somewhere. At the end of the line, another Jerry guard would open the parcel, and using his bayonet, jabbed about a three-quarter inch slit in the top of each can of perishables so you could not store them. However, to keep dirt out of the cans they punched holes in, we all learned to close the opening with a little oleo when we got back to the barracks. We found this also protected them against spoilage, for a while. Storage of such food, the Krauts felt, might tempt someone to make a break if several days' rations could be saved ahead.

Prunes or hot water became our alternating breakfast for the entire eighteen months that we were there. However, every once in a blue moon, we were served cooked barley and raisins for breakfast. This was the only decent thing we got. Now lunch was another story. The same soup every day, except once or twice a month we did get spuds and salmon, or spuds and corned beef. Our dinner was the same old soup again, except every two or three weeks we had spuds and salmon or corned beef and salmon. There was *no chow* on Saturday or Sunday for the evening meal, *not even hot water!* Here again, this was probably done to make us use any rations we had from Red Cross parcels, or you could go hungry—your choice!

Our folks at home were permitted to send us a personal parcel every sixty days, with a government permit, under the Geneva Convention. Most of those parcels were stolen by the Krauts in transit. Yet at home they had sent one every sixty days, I later learned! To make matters even worse, our folks at home got notice from our government that the Germans were immediately confiscating any prisoner parcels having markings on the outside such as "V for Victory," "Win the War," or any other victory slogans. Regular mail to the camp averaged three months in transit from the USA and airmail two months. Airmail letters *from* the camp to the USA were not permitted until about July 1944. Even then it was impossible because the Krauts wouldn't give us money due, so we couldn't use Luftposte and they knew it!

No letters or cards could be written by us, unless we used the required letter form or postal card that the Germans issued periodically. Anything else that was used was destroyed, as were the required forms if the writing was illegible or went beyond the printed lines. Supposedly, the Germans were to have issued from two to four letter forms and cards periodically. I never saw but a few of either in the possession of any POW. During March, April and May of 1944 letter forms and cards were not issued. But two weeks later, several thousand were printed when the Germans got word that the Protective Power was paying the camp a visit.

Because of censorship and processing, incoming mail often took four months for delivery. The Germans just looked for everything and anything they could do to hurt us.

Conditions is Stalag 17-B were deplorable, and we faced many hardships and health hazards. Treatment there was never considered good, and the guards were very hateful.

Even the camp's officers showed very little consideration for our well being, ignoring the terms of the Geneva Convention. There were times when things even became brutal.

Treatment of POWs in Stalag 17-B and Stalag 2-B was determined to be worse than any of the other seventy-eight German POW camps known to exist. Many cases were recorded of POWs having been struck by pistols and rifle butts, some even with bayonets. When the American compounds were first opened, it took a few months before the German Commandant would give an interview to Kenneth Kurtenbach, our MOC (Man of Confidence), to register protests on the poor conditions that prevailed throughout the camp.

When protests were given in writing they were ignored for weeks at a time before the Commandant would reply.

During our first few months no one was issued eating utensils. Then one day, every third man was issued a bowl and a spoon. The rest of us continued to use empty Klim cans (powdered milk cans) for bowls and fashioned spoons from Klim cans, as well as drinking mugs from Oleo cans.

The German Commandant was Oberst Kuhn, a hateful son of a bitch. It was my guess that he was a hard-line soldier of the old school and no doubt of the high Prussian variety, as he was completely uncooperative and unreasonable.

We did have other officers, also part of the camp command. One by the name of Major Eigl was reasonable at times. However, Eigl, being an officer in the Luftwaffe, caused friction with the others, who were all Wehrmacht; this gave him very little power, although he did try a little to be cooperative.

One day we were told to take everything we wanted to keep when we left Stalag 17-B and assemble outside in the compound. Naturally all of us wondered if we were leaving this place and we remained suspicious. Once we were all outside, German soldiers entered the barrack and began a search, but when we returned nothing had been taken.

On the following day we received the same orders, to which we again complied and nothing was touched this time, either. When the same order was given on the third day, we decided not to play this game any longer and most of us left everything in the barracks and went out to the compound to wait, as the Krauts made their search.

This was just what those bastards were waiting for. German guards entered one barracks after another and took food, clothing and anything they wanted.

Some things taken were of no use to anyone except us. But life as a POW would be more difficult without them, so that would be reason enough for the Krauts to take them.

Then other German soldiers brought in wagons, loaded them up with our goods and drove away. Kurtenbach protested to the Protective Power, and they convinced the German Commandant to return everything. Even though the Commandant agreed to do this, it was nearly impossible to comply once the goods were out of the camp.

One day it had been discovered that the camp kitchen had been broken into and a few hundred packs of cigarettes were stolen along with nearly three-hundred Red Cross parcels. We all knew the Krauts did it since they had the keys to the kitchen door and they loved those American cigarettes. How obvious can you be? As usual, when our MOC made a protest to the Commandant it was passed off lightly once again.

Then in September, 1944, Kurtenbach was informed by the International Red Cross that a few freight cars containing Red Cross parcels would be coming our way sometime in October. Although they did arrive, the Commandant never informed Kurtenbach of their arrival or even had them unloaded!

Instead, as Kurtenbach learned from the International Red Cross, the Commandant claimed he had been given orders to send the cars to another town where the parcels were stored in a warehouse.

I also heard stories that the train had been bombed by our aircraft and the Red Cross parcels were totally destroyed, all of which were lies.

Later, when the parcels were recovered, it was noted that a few of the cases had been pilfered, and all of this delay caused more hardship for us, as there were only about three-thousand parcels left in the camp.

During one night, in the winter of 1944, two men trying to escape were discovered in an unauthorized area, just outside of their compound. Both of these men instantly threw up their hands to surrender, yet the guards immediately opened fire, shooting both men where they stood. One of them died instantly and the other, fortunately, had only been wounded in the leg.

While the injured man was on the ground a guard ran up to him and shot him again. Then the guard wheeled around and wildly opened fire into one of the barracks, as if to show his contempt for all POWs because of this incident. As a result of the guard's crazy actions, one of the bullets he fired into the barracks struck another POW lying in his bunk, wounding him seriously.

The Germans would not permit other American POWs to bring the dead man inside the compound for burial or allow anyone to go near the wounded POW, who had to just lie there for several hours before permission was granted to give him medical attention.

During December of 1944, more freight cars arrived with more Red Cross food parcels. As I recall, every one of these had been broken into, pilfered, and many cases of the parcels had been stolen.

Chapter Seven

After talking to many people over the years, I am certainly convinced that most people in this country haven't the slightest idea what life as a POW is like. They seem to think being a POW is sort of like being in jail in the USA. Sadly, the conditions were so poor for a POW, there is no comparison!

Rats ran around the floor at night, and you could hear them fighting and squealing. One night, one even ran into a small table where some of us sat to eat, moving it a few inches. When Charlie Dyer and I heard the sliding noise of the table, we wondered just how big these rats must be.

In each half of the barracks were two small chimneys, evenly spaced apart. They each had a firebox near the bottom. These were meant for a small fire to heat the barracks. We got a little coal just once, maybe twice, during the entire eighteen months we were there, but I never saw any more. Yet claims were made that we received fifty-four pounds of coal a week, more B.S.! But these "fireplaces" were used every day by some of us to make hot water for a "brew" or mix some concoction somebody dreamed up using food from home or something in the Red Cross parcels—or both! Many of the guys even formed "combines" of 2 to 5 men, pooling all their foodstuffs from home and Red Cross parcels. Then they each took turns making the meal for the whole combine. The idea went over well and I guess seemed to "stretch" the food, plus someone else made your chow much of the time. The fuel for these fires came from Red Cross cartons that were torn up and saved and any other cardboard you could scrounge up in your travels to visit other barracks. Any wood was always welcome, if you could find it! Some of the barracks gradually lost their front porches, board by board, which undoubtedly went for "brew material," as we called it. This always made the Krauts furious and raving mad, but they could never seem to find out who did it.

We were all complaining to each other each time a parcel came from home about all the "dumb" stuff that was sent to us by our families. I found out after the war that our families were sending what the Office of Economic Warfare, Washington, D.C., advised on a list it had sent to our homes. I was absolutely appalled when I opened these cartons and amongst the foodstuffs and personal items were Chiclets, rootbeer Lifesavers, cinnamon, toothpicks, gum, candy, and worst of all—a necktie! Now this parcel could not exceed eleven pounds, so all this "dumb" stuff kept other *good* things from being sent.

In addition to this, a form from the same office states that the International Red Cross, through the American Red Cross, is now delivering parcels weekly to American POWs. Nothing could have been further from the truth! Red Cross parcels were given to us at very irregular intervals by the Germans, with the excuse being that our planes destroyed the train they were on and the townspeople took them. Or the trucks were shot up by our planes, etc., all just plain B.S.—they kept the parcels! Oddly enough, one of the guys in the barracks did receive a tobacco parcel from home and upon opening it, discovered a box of cigars inside that had been hit by machine-gun fire, cutting every one in half, or worse!

My first personal parcel from home came November 8, 1944, just about three weeks short of one year as a POW, which was December 1, 1943. The next one came December 19, 1944, then another around Christmas of 1944, and the last one on March 3, 1945. As per regulations, these parcels could not weigh over eleven pounds and could not be over eighteen inches long, nor over forty-two inches length and girth combined. Also, two license labels had to be acquired from the government for each parcel sent. Only one parcel could be shipped every sixty days and two tobacco parcels (three cartons of cigarettes or one hundred cigars to each parcel) in the same period.

The months rolled by as everyone tried to adjust to this new way of life. Not everyone did, unfortunately. I remember one Kriegie who began walking the barracks back and forth from one end to the other constantly until it was time for lights out. This went on day after day. Then one day, he rushed out the back door and ran for the fence. Hurdling the warning wire, he jumped onto the fence and screamed to the guard, "Shoot me, shoot me, I can't take it anymore!" There was one quick burst of machine-gun fire, and it was all over.

Other POWs who caused a ruckus were put in the "boob" (cooler) for a few days or more till they cooled down. The boob was the usual very confining little hut used for solitary confinement in any kind of weather for those considered unruly or breaking the rules.

Every now and then the doors, front and back, would fly open and armed guards would charge in blowing whistles and yelling, "Raus! Raus!" ("Out! Out!"), chasing us through the back of the barracks to the outside. There we stood, sometimes in the rain or snow and cold, not permitted to move from the area. We couldn't even use the latrine. If you had to "go," there was a huge hole in the ground nearby, which I believe had been dug to bury some trash, but I'm not sure anymore. Guards stood facing us about fifty feet away in a long line, maybe twenty feet apart, with Schmeisser machine guns pointed at us threateningly. There we stood, sometimes for hours, as the Krauts went through our barracks searching for what they could find to call contraband. Mostly it seemed they looked for crystal sets. These were frequently acquired by trading American cigarettes through the fence with the guards or other nationalities. Also, they looked for cans of food unpunched by the bayonet and quickly confiscated them.

We all took our turn on the crystal sets, lying awake at night to catch the war news on BBC. There were always a few crystal sets around the camp. Those that the Jerries found seemed to always be replaced. In the morning, all the "listeners" would turn in what they could remember of the news. It was pitch-black and any lights from matches would attract attention, so you would just have to get the gist of things. Then this information was combined with the others into a bulletin, which a runner took around to each barracks randomly the next day and read aloud to everyone. One man stood by each door watching for guards, just in case.

Between the front and back section of the barracks was a masonry-built room with running water, cold only, and a bare cement floor. The supported waterline was at about shoulder level, with faucet heads spaced along it. The excess water ran down a large, galvanized gutter arrangement. This was where you washed, did laundry by hand, etc. However, water was only available four hours a day and there were no laundry tubs and no heat, just like the barracks. Scrubbing clothes in the gutters of the washroom was a painful task, and I rubbed my knuckles raw each time and they took days to heal. Wintertime was even worse, trying to use regular soap and ice-cold water. Sometimes we would soak the clothes a few days in a canvas bag with soap chips. These bags had been given to us by the International YMCA. It worked rather well since it was round, about twelve inches across and about eighteen inches high, although it had to be rolled down some.

The YMCA was prompt to fill requisitions for sports equipment, but there was always considerable delay in getting approval from the German Commandant.

I guess one of the most difficult things I did there was to try to take a shower in the wintertime. This meant going into that washroom on that bare cement floor, turning the faucet around so it pointed up, and then trying to stand under it. An empty can with holes in the bottom, tied to the upside-down faucet, served as a shower head. The ice-cold water was almost unbearable and I wanted to scream out loud, it was so agonizing.

One of the three windows in the room had been torn out, frame and all, for "brew" material no doubt. As I tried to withstand the icy water, I noticed that the empty window opening had icicles hanging from it. The bitter-cold air and icy water were just more than I could bear, so I called it quits; I just couldn't continue.

About every six weeks, they marched us barrack by barrack to the "delouser." Here we were shoved like cattle into a shed of some sort with a dirt floor, to wait. The way they forced us in always incited our guys and they pushed back, which in turn riled the Jerries, who brought out their bayonets and rifle butts. Eventually, four or five guards would throw their weight against the door, closing and locking it. From here, it took about a half hour before we were let into the "undressing room." After undressing, you put all of your clothing on a hanger. Getting in a line, you handed them to someone who put them in the delousing oven, where cyanide pellets were placed to kill the fleas and any other lice. I saw this oven as a grim reminder of what it was probably used for in 1938–40, since this had been a concentration camp then. Next our hair was shaved off, not with a razor, but with electric clippers that would take it right down close to the scalp. Now came the shower. There was a Frenchman in charge who turned the water on and off by the clock. I believe he gave us one minute to soap and rinse. If the time was up and you still had soap on you—tough!

In another small room, we stood in line again, waiting to be inspected for lice. Those who had them were given a blue ointment to rub in the crotch area. It sure killed them, but it also felt like it was burning the skin off to boot, so many of the fellas said. As we stood naked, waiting, I noticed numerous battle scars on some of the others, plus we all had flea bites and sores of other kinds. Shortly, we left and entered a cold, large room that reeked with cyanide gas from the clothes of the previous group who had dressed and left for the outside. The floor in this room was muddy and so filthy that if you forgot your wooden clogs, you better hope you could borrow a pair. Even though you tried to dress quickly to get out of the fumes, your head would begin to ache. Some felt sick and on occasion even passed out.

Once outside, our clothes still smelled heavily of cyanide, even in the open air. It seemed like we were waiting forever to have the guards march us back. During the long wait, we were next to the compounds of Russian and Italian POWs. Every now and then onions would come flying over the fence to us from the gathering crowd, but never a word was said by either side. They were expecting cigarettes in return. There was no way to see where the onions came from but once the guard noticed it and took his gun off of his shoulder and looked ready to use it, this quickly stopped. I remember once when an onion hit a German guard and that really "steamed" him, as everyone laughed. Once a Russian was shot and killed reaching through the fence for a pack of cigarettes!

Chapter Eight

Months later, during the warm weather, we had just gone through this same procedure at the delouser and were all standing outside. We all noticed an Italian soldier sitting in an open window at the end of the barracks, with one leg propped up. Out of the blue, he called out, "Hiya, fellas, how's New York?"

We were all so astounded to hear this, we laughed at first. Then someone yelled to him, "Are you from New York?"

"Yeah!" he replied.

Then one of our guys yelled back, "Why the hell didn't you stay there?"

The answer came back, "I wish I had!"

Another cried out, "What part of New York are you from?"

"Brooklyn!" was the reply. This of course brought tumultuous boos. Then everyone laughed, including the Italian soldier.

The showers were okay, but we all hated that delouser routine. Finally, some of the guys put margarine and sand in their hair, which not only jammed the clippers, but the sand also rendered them useless. Another blade only did the same. But some of us got a haircut before that happened.

The fleas and lice were getting so bad in December of '43, just after we arrived, that it took one of our camp spokesman from the barracks we called the "White House" to talk to the camp Commandant, Captain Eigle (shortly to become a Major), and another camp officer, Captain Poletti, that an epidemic of typhus could break out if something was not done. At first the captain was difficult until it was pointed out that his guards could get it, too, which meant they would spread it all through Austria. That did it! Soon each barracks, one by one, was fumigated while we stopped over at an empty one for a day or so. Then we all took our blankets, clothes, etc. and under heavy guard, marched out the main gate to the delouser. There our things were given the cyanide treatment, and of course we were deloused, too. When that was done, we were allowed back into our regular barracks. I believe this was the time we not only had our heads shaved, but had to choose a buddy and then help each other shave what you couldn't reach of your "privates" yourself.

Each POW was entitled to pay at the rate of $1.63 a month. Needless to say, no one ever got this money because the Krauts claimed it was used to reimburse their government for making sundry items such as pencils, razor blades, soap paper, etc. available in the canteen. Bullshit, there was *never a canteen of any sort in the camp!* It was pretty obvious that the Germans just kept the money and made up this story.

Saving cardboard from Red Cross cartons, some of those interested in theatrics used half of one of the empty barracks to make a theater, calling it "The Cardboard Playhouse."

Those men in charge of entertainment traded with the French for wigs, dresses, makeup, and other clothing for our playhouse. I don't know how they procured all of the well-known Broadway plays we put on, unless it was through the YMCA. Using this material, we put on shows regularly for the rest of the camp. I was in twenty-six different plays while I was there, as a female impersonator in every play except one! I guess my biggest role was as a female in the big Broadway hit, "Front Page"! Oddly enough, even the guys in my own barracks didn't recognize me once I was made up and had on a wig and a dress. At least they never said anything. But then, I never told them I was in those plays either! We kept the plays running continuously by rehearsing one play during the day and putting a different one on at night. I finally got the lead in one, which we never put on because we broke camp and headed west.

There were other times that musical groups entertained all of the Kriegies. For a while our ball turret gunner, Bill Rasmussen, and his "Day Dreamers" took the stage, much to everyone's liking. We also had some comedy talent, too, along with hillbilly music and skits. Most nights you could find a Jerry guard standing along the back wall somewhere. I was never quite sure if he was there to see the show or play spy. Maybe both!

As the months wore on, tempers would fly over almost nothing and a fistfight started. To help solve this, it was usually broken up until they got the gloves on. The fight was stopped mostly because if any damage was done with bare fists, medical or dental help could be a problem. This led a group of fellows to build a boxing ring. Next came regulation matches as additional entertainment, even with a referee. A basketball court was made and teams formed, along with a few softball teams. There were also various educational opportunities that had been organized by T/Sgt. Haddon. After acquiring and organizing a staff, classes were offered in many subjects. There was photography, law, music, economics, American history, and others, plus several languages. These things, along with the Allied armies' progress in our direction, kept morale in the camp good as well as improving the mind.

Tunnel digging was the favorite pastime of a number of Kriegies. The biggest problem was what to do with the dirt brought out of the tunnel. To begin with, the barracks were built up off the ground a couple feet or more, so the Jerries could see under them easily. For a while the dirt could be scattered around evenly under the center of the barracks, or even taken away to another barracks and scattered underneath where no tunnel was underway. It took a while before the Krauts caught on to this, but they did. What baffled them the most was there was no tunnel being dug under the barracks where the dirt seemed to be accumulating. Then, for some time the dirt was brought up to the washroom and flushed down the drain. Somehow the Jerries got wise to this and shut the water off except for an hour or two each morning, noon, and evening. Trying to scatter the dirt outside would not work either, due to the different color and texture of the soil. All the tunnel digging made the Jerries so nervous, they finally tore down one of the barracks that they thought was too close to the fence (about seventy-five feet or more). It seemed every time a tunnel was underway, the Jerries would suddenly show up at the right barracks and "discover" it. Once the tunnel was discovered, it was immediately smashed in and closed, plus those involved and caught were immediately sent to the "boob." So it was pretty obvious that we had a "mole" in our midst.

The mole was quickly discovered, a Kraut in clothes like ours, who had been under suspicion for some time anyway because of his accent. Now it was a case of steering clear of him with any conversation, except some of the guys liked to needle him and let him know we were on to him. Some of the POWs gave him the name "Abbie the Mole," which he soon realized, for everywhere he went you would hear somebody shout, "Hey, Abbie!" or "Abbie the mole!" Prior to all this, he had tried to mingle with POWs in different barracks but he seemed to stand out like a sore thumb with his mannerisms and accent. This didn't work with any of us, and before long, he was back in uniform snooping around outside for tunnels.

No one ever escaped from Stalag 17-B, although many tried and were either shot or placed in solitary confinement for thirty days or more for all their efforts. Even so, there was one

Kriegie named Lee "Shorty" Gordon who became a frequent topic of conversation. It seems Shorty was a POW in Stalag 7A, Mooseburg, Germany, when he learned that the American POWs were to be moved to Stalag 17-B at Krems, Austria. Having heard there would be SS guards there, he was leery about his chances of escape once he was in that camp. So Shorty managed to switch his identity with an Australian, complete with POW tags. Dropping the "Shorty" part, the Australian became just Lee Gordon from then on. The Krauts I don't believe ever realized it and the "other" Shorty Gordon, now known just as Lee Gordon, took his place with the Americans. Meanwhile, the real Lee Gordon, now an Aussie, mixed in with the remaining British POWs at 7A and later managed to escape.

The name "Shorty" had to be forgotten as Shorty was only 5'2" tall and his replacement was several inches taller. I never figured how he got through picture check, but then again it only shows your face and shoulders, so somehow he did. I knew the "new" Lee Gordon very well since he worked with all of us who took roles in the various plays put on at the Cardboard Playhouse. Consequently, I worked very closely with him for all of those twenty-six plays I mentioned earlier, since we all saw him as our director. But here is the irony of this whole story. While I was still in training back in the States, our class had the good fortune to listen to the exploits of a U.S. Army Air Corps sergeant who was an aerial gunner and after being shot down and taken prisoner, escaped and made his way back to the Allies. His name was Lee "Shorty" Gordon! At that time his name meant nothing to me, of course, but what a shock when I met the other Shorty in Stalag 17-B and learned the full story. Many of the other POWs in the camp knew of Shorty's daring escape and his replacement, but they did not know about my experience with the real Shorty back in the States. Just try to imagine the odds of my ever meeting both of these fellows like this: It meant being in the right training program, in the right school, at the right time, in the right class. Then being sent to England to fly with the Eighth Air Force, getting shot down, and of the dozens and dozens of POW camps, ending up in Stalag 17-B with the other Lee Gordon. Now that's odds!

We also had twenty-one air raids in the vicinity from December 1943 through March 1945, mostly by the USAF. Some RAF and once the USAF strafing with some P-51 Mustangs joined with USSR fighters. This was on March 26, 1945. Two or three P-38s buzzed our camp on April 1, 1945, as they were making their turn to strafe Krems about two miles below us. One of the guards in a tower shot at one of the planes with his rifle as it passed overhead, and we all laughed aloud.

There were night raids, too. These were done by the RAF, of course. I had been told that the Limeys thought we were crazy to fly missions in broad daylight—at night was the only way! Well, maybe for them, but not for us! Formation flying was out of the question at night, so single bombers spaced minutes apart was the only way. We could hear the planes as they droned overhead and could only try to see something out of the windows. Go outside to watch, and the guards would surely shoot you! One night, we saw bright orange flares come down, which seemed to mark out the camp. We thought this was so they would not bomb the camp by mistake. The planes seemed to go back and forth above us for about an hour. We could not see any planes in the pitch-black night as they all had exhaust shields on. Then all was quiet and the "all clear" was sounded, so we decided there was no raid after all.

Three nights later it was a different story, however, as the airfield east of the camp was bombed. This time the Jerries let us go out to the trenches in the back. You could hear the exploding bombs, see flashes from flak guns being fired and their shells exploding high in the night sky. One of the planes we heard flying around must have been a German night fighter. All of a sudden we heard machine-gun fire, and a bright explosion burnt a hole in the pitch-black sky as the burning plane come down near us. Others came down in flames that night, too, but there was no way we could determine if they were German or British. I guess Vienna was the target on this raid, judging by the "Christmas Tree" marker flare that was dropped. One plane after another droned overhead, headed for the flare markers and the target marker, the "Christmas Tree." Bombs exploded continuously with all their fury, bright flashes and thunder, which we could only see above the skyline due to the terrain.

A few days later, someone in our compound was talking to a Limey in the British compound. It seems that two of the British airmen shot down that night were in his barracks. They told him that just three nights before when they hit that nearby airfield, we were almost all blown to hell! The Pathfinders had "laid" our camp out as the target. That's what those bright orange flares were we saw through the windows and didn't realize then what was happening. At the last moment their "Pathfinder" realized the mistake and signaled their bombers, who were already making their run, to turn back. Every plane had a map showing the location of known POW camps, so I guess somebody suddenly woke up! Thank God!

One day in the fall of 1944, a Me 262 German jet passed overhead. This was the first operational jet fighter in the history of aviation. The air war over Europe would no doubt have been much different for the Allies had Hitler realized the potential of this airplane. Instead, he attempted to make a lot of variations of it, including a bomber and a night fighter. Consequently, as a result of this policy, out of more than 1,400 Me 262s built, less than 25 percent of them became operational. Since this all took place during the waning months of the war, their presence had very little effect.

We were all outside in the open area of the compound at the time and none of us ever heard of a jet airplane in those days, so when those engines roared overhead, everyone made a mad dash for the trenches. Even when we looked up and saw it, everyone kept saying, "What is it? What is it?" This plane could do 540 mph! We all ran for the trenches because the noise was that of a salvo load of bombs coming down. Falling bombs make a rushing noise much like coal going down a chute.

I guess the most excitement came the day 110 of our heavies (B-24s) bombed Krems. Standing out back, we could actually see the bombs as they came out of the bomb bay, falling toward earth by the hundreds. Most people seem to think bombs whistle as they fall, but that is only if they are rigged for it or the plane is, such as the German JU-87 Stuka dive bomber. It had a sort of high-pitched siren on the undercarriage, which screamed as it dove on the target, terrorizing those below about to be bombed. "Whistling" bombs are for the movies.

Being the enterprising individuals they are, Americans always automatically systemize things for their benefit. One POW was chosen by the others to be camp leader and he had a staff. These officials of ours all lived in the part of one barracks we all knew as the "White House." Only we referred to our "head man" as the "Camp Leader." In due time an election was held to see if we wanted a change, should any other POWs want the jobs. I don't recall any changes, except maybe one of the staff stepping down for some reason or another.

Probably one of the most interesting things to come about was the establishment of our "Monetary Unit," the D-bar. The D-bar came in the Red Cross parcels and was a highly-concentrated bar of chocolate, a good three-fourths of an inch thick and weighing four ounces. It was compressed so hard it usually had to be broken over the edge of a table or the like on one of the dividing lines, two squares at a time. It was so rich the label

111

even cautioned: "Do not consume more than two squares in a 30 minute period!" Try it and you will be sick, that you can be sure. Actually, under "in field" conditions, a D-bar could be considered a day's rations, to be eaten two squares at a time for each of three meals. It seemed to be all pure stuff and never spoiled. I once heard that it took sixteen Hershey chocolate bars to make one D-bar. Everyday summer heat didn't bother it either; it was still just as hard and stable. All the foregoing factors made the D-bar the most acceptable commodity in the parcel to everyone in the camp, and it became our monetary unit. Gradually the value of each food commodity attained a D-bar value, depending upon supply and demand.

*(A D-bar value listing can be found in the back of this text.)

Inflation also set in. A year or so later when many "new" POWs were brought into the camp and put in the "new compound" the Jerries had just opened, prices went wild. The new guys, picking up on our system, wanted more D-bar value for their items. This in turn drove the "asking price" of the items up, so the next time around everything was higher. My, doesn't this sound familiar? Some fellows made a business of this bartering plan. Every day it seemed someone in the camp came around "hawking" some food item with the price slightly inflated. He would work his way through every barracks looking for that one POW who would buy. Doing this every day with different items, little by little his "bank" value increased, and so it went.

The months grew longer, and it seemed we were going to be here forever. Then one day, the word came down that the Russians were gaining on all fronts, heading west. It was a well-established fact that the last thing any German wanted was to be captured by the Russians. The atrocities committed by the Germans as they made their way to Stalingrad were deeply burned into the mind of every Russian soldier, making them a vicious foe as they gallantly fought their way through Germany and into Berlin.

The following day, the Russians were rumored to be about thirty kilometers from Krems and fighting their way to St. Polten. We knew they couldn't be far away, for at night we could see the big guns flashing in the sky, so it was only a question of time before they would be at our camp.

Later the word quickly spread that a guard had said an order had come down for each camp Commandant to execute all of the POWs! There were always so many rumors, it was difficult to decide which one to believe. In any case, we kept alert, waiting. As I recall, some sort of plan had been devised for us to go into action in case the Germans attempted to carry out such an order, but nothing happened.

Instead, the Jerries now told our camp leader to get the men ready to evacuate, claiming they were moving us some distance from Krems to save us from the Russians, but we all knew the real reason was that the Germans feared capture by the Russians. So our camp leader, Kenneth Kurtenbach, ordered us to "get ready" but to refuse to leave unless the Germans threatened to shoot us. Once all the guys heard the word "evacuate," the whole camp was in an uproar. There were bonfires everywhere day and night, probably burning what they couldn't carry and didn't want the Jerries to get. Also, it was hoped that all of these fires and other forms of resistance would prevent our being moved. Besides, international law made it illegal to move POWs, considering the circumstances. We were hardly up to it after being on starvation rations for a year and a half. But since it appeared we would be heading east toward the Allies, it was decided that we should go with the guards. The guards were few enough with each group that they could have been quickly overpowered later, if need be.

A small office the Jerries kept was quickly broken into. I guess under different circumstances it would have been called

Nr: 100.478	Mc DOWELL Gerald		BARACKE: 18 A
	GEB. DATUM: 17.4.23.	AMERIK. MATR. Nr: 33.480.463	
	FÜHRUNG:	BEURTEILUNG:	
	STRAFEN:	STRAFBARE HANDLUNGEN:	

This is a copy of my file card and "mug" shot taken by the Germans at Stalag 17-B in December 1943. It was kept on file by them for periodic prisoner checks.

"looting," since the place was ransacked and files and POW records were taken out and thrown on the bonfire. By now, you could see that the Germans had lost control of the camp and didn't really seem to care. It seemed everybody was scurrying in all directions. One fellow POW, rooting through the Stalag 17-B files, found his ID and picture card made by the Germans, and spotting mine, too, saw to it that I got it for a souvenir. I have it yet today, now in a frame along with my POW dog tags.

The next day was April 8, 1945, and we had been told we would rise at 6:00 A.M. and leave at 7:00, so everyone was trying hard mentally to prepare for this forced march. How far it would be we did not know, nor how well we could take it either. Fortunately, the weather was dry that day, unlike the rainy day before, but it was cold. However, it did warm up some by noon.

Chapter Nine

It was now time to leave this godforsaken place, leaving behind only *one* POW, who died from natural causes many months earlier. He received a military gun salute from the Jerries as all the POWs, standing in ranks, saluted the passing coffin. There were other American POWs who were shot while trying to escape, but they never received a military funeral.

The Krauts divided the 4,200 of us up into eight groups with five hundred men to a group, plus or minus a few, and out the gate we went, heading west, with a few miles between each group.

*(I kept a detailed diary of this 281-mile march, day by day, and a copy of it can be found at the end of this story.)

About three hundred of the men did stay behind because they couldn't walk and some others had bribed the Jerries so they could stay. That was a bad move, I later learned, because they spent most of April in the air raid trenches, but they were liberated on May 9, 1945, by the Russians.

There were about eight German guards to each five hundred men. As we marched west, all I could think of was each step was a step toward freedom—I hoped! Some of the POWs spent a short time in Stalag 17-B, but most of us were there one and a half years. A couple of POWs had been in other Stalags first and then here for the full time, making them POWs about two years or more in this rotten place. Even in our condition, we walked the pants off the guards. I guess we were fired up and feeling it was soon to be over, our spirits raised. We walked about fifty minutes, then rested for ten. We could have easily overpowered our guards, but the word came down that as long as we were going west, stay with it. Also, the uniformed guards with rifles could be a bit of protection for us against any riled-up citizens seeing us go by. The next day, April 9, a rumor came down that the Russians had bombed Krems and Stalag 17-B had been hit, too, but no American POWs had been injured.

As we marched that 281 miles through the hilly country of towns and villages, there were some unforgettable sights I will remember the rest of my life. For instance, a small group of Jews being herded along the dirt road were apparently not moving fast enough to suit one Nazi soldier, so he slammed one Jew in the head a few times with his rifle butt. As our group passed by the spot, I saw a very large pool of fresh blood on the road and knew that person must be dead. I didn't see a body, but they probably threw it over the small wall along the side of the road.

We also passed by various concentration camps that were just like Buchenwald, Dachau, Belsen, and the like. I can't say for sure which camps they were, as we were not near the gates to see any names. But they were surely the same, for as we came on top of a rise, I could clearly see into one of them. Watching as we marched along, I saw a pile of bodies in striped uniforms stacked up like firewood and two guards just then throwing two more bodies up on the pile. Many other prisoners were laboring in the camp. Anyone falling down was whipped until he got up or died on the spot from the whip, or maybe even shot where he went down. As we moved on, we came upon a wagon being pushed along by about four or six prisoners, apparently from the same camp. They looked like they had been starved, and could hardly stand up. They, too, wore those same black-and-white striped uniforms. The weather made the road so soft it was almost muddy, and those few men were trying to move this wagon along as it kept sinking in the soft ground. A couple of armed guards accompanied them, watching intently as if looking for an excuse to shoot.

I looked closely at one man as they passed by. He looked more dead than alive, his eyes sunken back in his head. His mouth hung open and he had a fixed, straight-ahead stare as he tried desperately to keep the wagon moving. I am certain all the other men were the same way, as well as those in the camp below. How in the name of humanity could the Germans call this a part of war.

A couple of weeks later, I believe it was, we heard the engine of a single aircraft above. It was a small German reconnaissance plane called a "Storch" (German for Stork). Suddenly another aircraft appeared on the scene, a USAF P-51 Mustang. It seemed he was flying in to look us over to see who we were, then he spotted the Storch. With that, the Mustang made a power dive on the Storch. Down came the Mustang with guns blazing away. To our amazement, at the last possible moment the Storch made a snappy side turn, and the Mustang with its 300 or 400 mph speed was unable to turn and went roaring right by the Storch. But the Mustang was not to be denied. High in the sky, far away, he turned and started another power dive pass. Again he came in with guns blazing and again the Storch turned away just in time. This went on for some time, and after about five passes, the Mustang made one final pass over us, waggled his wings in recognition, and decided he had better things to do.

On April 11, we marched through a town loaded with German SS troops who looked viciously at us. Even our guards were afraid of them, so we all put it in high gear to get away from there as fast as possible, trying to ignore them as we went.

On April 12, I became very ill in the middle of the night.

I didn't get much sleep and became awfully weak and was sweating heavily. It was no doubt dysentery from the water I got from a stream where we had stopped for a break, and I hadn't quite boiled it. The next morning I felt weaker, and was just about ready to throw in the towel. Even Charlie Dyer said at our reunion in 1988 that he thought then I was surely going to die, I was that bad. Anyway, I convinced the medics to let me put my pack on the wagon. This made it possible for me to stay on my feet, but I moved slowly and gradually fell far behind in the group, feeling like I would fall over any minute as I staggered on. I knew if I did fall and somebody didn't pick me up quickly and get me to the wagon we had, the Krauts would no doubt shoot me on the spot. But somehow I managed not to fall. It seemed like we would never stop for the day. When we finally did, I virtually collapsed in my tracks! Somehow I had been able to keep going and covered thirteen kilometers that day, I'll never know how! The following day I was a little stronger and able to cover the seventeen kilometers more like normal.

Also on this day, April 12, we got word that President Roosevelt had died.

Since we only traveled the back roads and through the foothills of the Alps, the going was tough at times and all of this hilly country was beginning to tell on most everyone's feet. Sometimes it poured down rain, but we still kept going. I can remember during one of the blizzard-like snows, I couldn't see a thing it was so blinding. All I did was watch the fellow's heels in front of me, and shielding my eyes, just kept trudging along. Had he gone over a cliff, I guess I would have, too!

The long trek took its toll on the German guards, too. During the march, four died. One fell off a wagon and broke his neck, and another was "accidentally" killed when someone pushed him in front of a truck. The others I don't know about.

We had marched 281 miles in eighteen days through fifty-

119

seven towns and had been forced to sleep outdoors in all kinds of weather. But there were three or four nights when we slept in barns, cowsheds, and the like. We eventually ended up at Braunau, which is divided by the Inn River, half in Austria and half in Germany. Also, it is the town where Hitler was born!

Here we were on top of this very large hill, thick with trees, and the Krauts said this was our destination. So everyone started to build lean-tos, using long-needle pine boughs for the roof. It was really a shame how the bark was stripped from dozens and dozens of trees about six or eight feet up from the bottom, for they surely died later. Bark laid on the roof of the lean-tos like curved tiles, one up, one down, made a perfect shield from the never ending rain. Interestingly enough, there were no escape attempts while we were here, for we all knew our troops were not far away. Along about now we all received a Red Cross parcel, which was brought in by trucks. A few days later more were issued, but one for every five men.

I won't go into any more detail here on what followed in the next few days as it is covered in later text you will read. Also, some things may be repeated for the purpose of continuity.

On Tuesday, May 1, I walked with another POW just out of the camp over to the edge of a high precipice overlooking the Inn River Valley. Here we saw an American tank with gun leveled, cautiously approaching a stone building. After some light machine-gun fire, they stopped the tank briefly, then let go with one round from the tank's gun. A soldier or two approached the building, saw it was empty, and moved on. It was almost like the movies. Here we are way up here watching the war progress. Naturally, the tank was not alone, but that was about all we could see from our vantage point.

The next day, May 2, 1945, was the greatest. A tank came clattering along the road and up the hill almost to the camp, under truce. A Nazi staff car with flags in the fender sockets

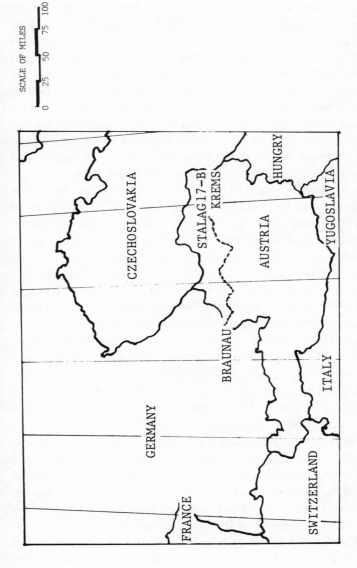

SCALE OF MILES

0   25   50   75   100

The broken line on the map from Krems to Braunau, Germany, shows the route of the 281 miles we covered on the forced march, as we followed the back roads in a zig-zag course through the foothills of the Alps for nineteen days to Braunau.

headed for the tank. The tank stopped short and a American captain climbed out. He went away from the tank at a right angle from the road, then walked parallel with the road toward the staff car. When he was across from it, he talked to them from that point, but never walked up to them. As he told us later, "You noticed I went off the side of the road a ways before heading toward that staff car. I told my gunner that I would go see what they wanted but to keep the tank's gun right on the radiator cap of the car. If anybody makes a move—fire!" He also mentioned that he didn't trust any of these "bastards" and they had come too far to make a wrong move now. Anyway, he came up under truce to talk to us, saying that the front line was moving too fast now for him to stay, but he would try to send trucks for us shortly. "But first," he said, "let's get some food up here to you and then we'll get you out!" At this point he jumped up on a big tree stump and shouted loudly to everyone, "Men, you are no longer prisoners of war, you are soldiers of the United States Army!" Which, of course, brought loud cheers from everyone. He also told us how lucky we were because his unit was suspicious of this hill and was sure that it was loaded with Krauts. So they were getting ready to call for "fire" to level it with 105mm guns just back of them a few miles, when he decided he wanted to run up and take a look first. Whew! Now wouldn't that have been a disaster after all that we had survived? After a few more words, he ran down to his tank and headed back down the hill to his unit.

The next day, we heard a couple of jeeps coming up the hill. As they pulled up, out jumps a lieutenant colonel, a master sergeant, and five privates. Their feet had hardly hit the ground when all the Krauts threw down their rifles, yelling, "Kamerad, Kamerad!" What was left of them who had not run off, or died on the road, surrendered to *seven* American soldiers, which immediately told me they had more than enough war. Even more so, they had feared capture by the Russians, who were closing from the East. Then the colonel barked out some orders, "Alright, round up the Krauts and if anybody argues or gives you any trouble, shoot 'em!" Standing near the American colonel was a German colonel and as they talked, the American master sergeant tapped the German colonel's arm and said, "I'll take your Luger now, Colonel." The colonel replied, "I wish to surrender my gun and troops formally." In a flash, the sergeant's .45 automatic leaped from its holster, the slide flew back, then forward, loading a round in the chamber as the sergeant shoved the automatic in the German colonel's side. Now this sergeant was not only stocky but looked rather athletic and had a rugged face and piercing, cold eyes. Glaring right into the German colonel's eyes, he said, "I'll take your Luger now, Colonel, or you'll drop right where you're standing!" There was no doubt in anyone's mind that he would have done just what he said, either. Once that .45 automatic hit the German colonel's belly, he couldn't give up his Luger fast enough.

Furthermore, the sergeant and the colonel had been together since the day they hit the beach at Normandy, and after coming this far, had no intention of putting up with this Kraut's nonsense. The next thing the German colonel comes up with is, "Colonel, I will expect you to take very good care of my men. As you can see, I have taken very good care of yours." Slowly looking around at all of us and seeing our condition and how we were struggling here, our colonel said in a soft, disgusted tone, "Yeah, like hell you have!"

Well, in no time at all the GIs rounded up the Krauts and made them "fall in" and throw their rifles in a pile. Now it was our turn. The colonel announced to everyone, "I understand that the lot of you men have been prisoners for a long time and that some of you had some bad experiences. So, if anybody has any scores to settle, there's the Krauts and there's the guns!" I dare say that a number of fellows moved forward, chose a Kraut and a rifle, and disappeared over the hill. In a while the GIs came back, alone! What they did or did not do, I can't say.

Along about this time there was a ruckus nearby and it seemed an American soldier had hold of a Hitler Youth kid, maybe about fourteen or fifteen years old. Just where he came from, I do not know. However, one of our POWs needed boots so the GI, who was well over six feet tall, told the Hitler Youth kid to take them off, three different times. Each time the kid all but spit in his face and yelled something in German that probably wouldn't be printable. With that, the GI drew his trench knife, reached down, and with a couple of quick slashes, cut the laces on the boots. This infuriated the youth and he stepped forward unleashing a terrific uppercut that sent the GI sprawling on his back. Everyone stood dumbfounded for a moment, but the GI got to his feet and went flying into the youth. Moments later some others pulled him off or he would have surely killed that boy with his trench knife, but then none of us could have cared less if he had. The Hitler Youth organization was rotten to the core and just as fanatic, barbaric and bloodthirsty as the German SS.

The rest of the Germans were taken down to the river and put to work building a pontoon bridge, even the officers, I heard.

The 13th Armored Division had now taken over the camp and had a couple of trucks trying to get rations to us, as we were now completely out. Most of the food brought in was confiscated from Branau below and took considerable time to collect, little by little. It was slow coming with only a couple of trucks to spare for carrying food, and with 4,200 hungry men, it didn't go far before the truck was empty again. The food was spread thin in order to give everyone a little. We were all quite hungry and rations from the Krauts were in short supply. Just before leaving Stalag 17-B we were given food from Red

Cross parcels, supposedly enough to last for seven days, and we all stretched it to the limit before it was gone. Still, on the march many of us resorted to trading with the civilians for some food once the Red Cross parcel supplies were exhausted. We also traded with some of the guards for food.

The American troops had also hoped to get enough trucks to move us, but the front lines were moving too fast and they had to keep up with the other divisions. I believe the same tank captain came back and said he was sorry for all the delay but the only way they could help right now was if we could march to a factory ten miles from here. It was in back of the lines, and arrangements would be made to get us out. He also added that he realized how weary we must all be by now and that we had marched enough in our condition (knowing of the 281 miles we covered since leaving Stalag 17-B at Krems), but this is the only thing he could do to help us right now. He stated further we would be inside to sleep where it was warm and dry, for a change. So with that we all saddled up, put our packs on our backs, and started the ten-mile trek in the rain. This was in the evening of Saturday, May 5.

Down the road we went, no formation, just free-step marching sort of all strung out along the road, a weary, weather-beaten, and hungry lot with determination to continue on. I'll never guess where the energy came from, but on we went mile after mile. I never stopped once in the whole ten miles to rest, and I only saw two or three others who did. It was interesting to note, too, how little noise there was among us as we pressed on: no singing, no laughing, and almost no conversation. I can only guess just what spurred everyone on. Reaching our destination, an aluminum factory at Ranshofen, we spread out on the floor. It sure was good to sleep inside where it was dry and warm; even though the floor was cement, it still was great. A little later, we were moved to better quarters for the night. I can't remember where, but my diary shows that we did move.

The next day, May 6, we were put on half-tracks and trucks and headed for Passau. I quickly grabbed a spot alongside of a .50 caliber Browning mounted on the half-track. There were still snipers and some holdouts around, and I wanted to be ready if need be; besides, that .50 caliber machine gun was my "baby!"

Eventually we stopped at Tutting Airfield, near Potting. Here we had to wait through the day until some C-47s showed up to take us out. The planes didn't show up, so we had to sleep out that night. Four of our crew chose a 10-in-1 case of rations for dinner. I believe this means the one case of food was to feed ten men. However, the four of us ate the whole thing. I don't remember about them, but I really got sick and had diarrhea. The food was just too drastic a change—which shows you can't eat decent food when you are use to eating "garbage!" I ate a whole can of baked ham and pineapple and it was worth it, sick or not!

The next day, Tuesday, May 8, as we sat waiting for the C-47s to arrive, a small German transport landed on the field and surrendered the plane and crew. This was of course a big surprise to everyone on the field. There were four crew members aboard and two Luftwaffe women. The American GIs quickly rounded them up and put them on a truck, but before they pulled away, a number of us jumped up on the truck to strip them of "souvenirs." I wasn't quick enough to grab any pistols, but I did get a fine decoration from one of the Kraut's tunics. It looked handmade: a swastika with a copper-looking wreath surrounding it and the usual red, white, and black strip plus a blue/gray outer trim. I didn't have a knife to cut it away but one of the other POWs heard me tell this Kraut to take off this decoration, whatever it was, which he wouldn't do. So my friend whipped out a knife as he said to me, "Do you want this?" With that, he quickly slashed the threads around it and handed it to me. Of course the Nazi strongly protested as he kept trying to hold on to it, at the same time ranting and raving.

But this only served to make it more valuable to me and I enjoyed seeing this bastard whine! I don't know what the decoration was but somebody thought the Kraut was Navy.

Shortly after this, the C-47s came in and we got aboard and took off for Nancy, France. GI trucks met the planes and took us to the center of Nancy. As we piled out of the trucks and walked up the street toward a diner, people saw how slovenly we looked and immediately crossed the street long before they were near us. Once in the diner, they fed us a good old GI meal as a French combo played "The Stars and Stripes Forever," which gave me goose pimples. As I looked across the table at Wingate, the top turret gunner, I saw tears rolling down his cheeks and I had to look away as I became choked up, too, just seeing him.

From here they put us on the old "40/8" (Forty and Eight) boxcars of WWI vintage, which meant forty men or eight horses to each car. Once aboard, we headed for Epinal, France. We pulled into Epinal around 5:00 A.M., and they immediately took us to a RAMP Reception Center (Recovered Allied Military Personnel) for processing. Here we were rehabilitated on a diet which took a few days to gradually help us adjust back to normal food. There were three large rooms with a strictly controlled diet for each one. I started off eating a soft diet, no seasoning of any sort and only small portions. After the second day, that agreed with me and I was sent to the second diet room for meals with slightly larger portions. Two days later, my stomach seemed ready to accept normal food if lightly seasoned, but certainly no rich food of any kind! Next came showers, delousing, and all new clothes. The others were burned, I think.

The next morning, May 11, Wingate, Comer, and I left on the first convoy to the train station. This time we were put on a *real* train. We were in day coaches, which had real "plushy" padding. As we rode along, I remember hearing speakers playing, "Drinking Rum and Coca-Cola." It was difficult to sleep sitting up in this day coach, but I didn't care. There were various stops along the way, which gave us a break off the train to stretch our legs. Pulling into a station about forty miles from Le Havre, France, we transferred to trucks and went a few miles down the road to a tent city named "Camp Lucky Strike." I heard someone say that there were 80,000 men here, all waiting to go home! I can believe it, too, with tents almost as far as the eye could see and about twenty-five men to a tent. There were also numerous blacktop roads running all through the area, making it a small town. Here's where we signed out for a furlough allowing us sixty days of "R&R" once we got home.

On Sunday, May 13, I sent a wire home to let everyone know I had been liberated. We had been here one week and it had been raining almost every day. We were all just waiting to be processed, have a medical, and get to the port of Le Havre, where a ship will take us home.

Tuesday, May 22, 1945: General Eisenhower came in on a C-47 to see how things were going.

On Friday, May 25, they gave us a physical, had processing, got a typhus shot, dog tags and filled out a bunch of papers, and we were interrogated. Something sticks in my memory about G-2 interrogation. We were strongly reminded that under military law, when we got home we were not to reveal or discuss with anyone anything about POW camp, treatment there, or any atrocities we saw or were involved in. I don't remember a time limit on this, but it was probably for as long as you were in the military, I presumed. Most of us didn't want to talk about it anyway, for who would understand what had happened.

Also, I learned I was eligible for a few more ribbons and battle stars. After all of this—back to waiting!

Chapter Ten

Finally, on June 5, trucks took us to Le Havre where we boarded the USS *Admiral Benson*, which looked like a troop ship. We sailed at near top speed as the ship was equipped with radar and could easily detect any submarines. Of course there was a complete blackout in effect. One day we came close to a mine and when a few riflemen were unable to hit the "horns" to set it off, a gunnery crew blew it up with their 40mm gun.

Then one night we had a close call with an iceberg when the water temperature dropped twenty degrees in thirty minutes, making everybody hold their breath. The engines were cut as we crept onward for some time, using sonar to find the iceberg. We lucked out again, as the temperature began to rise slowly and we soon resumed speed. About five or six days later, we were back in the United States and they sent us to Camp Kilmer, New Jersey.

All we had to do here was shower, chow up, and get our back pay. While I was standing in line at the mess hall, there was a newscaster from station WPEN, Philadelphia, who wanted to interview me on the air. This interview was a national broadcast, coast to coast! I didn't realize this until later. They even cut a record and sent me a copy.

My back pay was an eye-opener, too, as I received about eighteen months' pay in one lump! They kept their word at Kilmer, telling us we could go home once we were paid, and any further processing would be taken care of when we came back. We were only there about two or three days anyway, so it was home for sixty days TD (temporary duty).

While at home, those sixty days flew by fast and I still didn't feel just right, so I went over to Valley Forge Veterans Hospital for an extension. Under the circumstances, I was granted another thirty days. During my stay at home, I received a telegram from the government telling me that as soon as my leave expired, I was to report to Miami Beach, and then that changed later to San Antonio, Texas, for *"re-processing and re-assignment"!* I was absolutely flabbergasted to think I would be sent to the Pacific Theater for more combat duty after all this!

The thought of more duty preyed on my mind day after day, but I was determined I would face it and not run off to Canada like today's "yellow bellies." None of us ever wanted to go to war either, but when it's your turn and you do not go, someone else has to go in your place and if he is killed because you "yellow bellied" out, then you will have this to live with the rest of your life! Worse yet, your family and friends will never forget—never! I often wonder how these guys can live with this. But then, why should they care, since they ran off in the first place? No doubt they also feel, "It's better that you get killed than me!" I am thankful this attitude didn't prevail in our war days. I can honestly say I pray that those who ran off to Canada will *never* in their lifetime be allowed back in this country! Just how many others went in their place and died because of these "cowards" we will probably never know! They have certainly shown all Americans and the world just where their true allegiance lies. Amen!

When my ninety days' leave was up, I headed for Texas as ordered. The designation of the field at San Antonio was SADAAFPDC (San Antonio District Army Air Force Personnel Distribution Command). The place was jammed with former POWs, just about all Air Corps, I guess.

Apparently Command Headquarters, in devising the "point" system to discharge men returning from overseas, overlooked the fact that any POW would have very few points and could not be discharged under this system. Probably they never expected the thousands of POWs from the Air Corps, either. I believe the table started at 85 or 90 points and dropped 5 points at a time as men were discharged. Even so, overseas, combat, POW time, medals, etc., we never came close. I think I had about 45 or 50 points at the time. So here we all sat while they slowly lowered the points required as men were discharged elsewhere.

In the meantime, we had nothing to do and all day to do it. We used the recreation facilities, got haircuts, went to the movies, and wrote letters. Then suddenly one day the points dropped down to our range. Day after day, groups with the required number of points were ordered to assemble at the base theatre at a given time, and you can be sure *no one* was late for this one! First we got a pep talk from a high-ranking officer about how we had served our country at a time of great need and how it was time to get on with our lives and "good luck" to everyone. Then we each were called up on the stage, where he saluted each of us as we received our discharge papers and any medals we had coming. Then there was one last loud call of "AT-TEN-SHUN," and the whole theatre of men jumped to their feet as if one. Then came the one word everyone wanted to hear, "DIS–SMISSED!" and when I heard that word "Dismissed," I headed for the door. I never looked back in case someone had changed his mind and would be beckoning to me to come back! Naturally, they had been asking each of us if we wanted to sign up for the reserve, to which there was almost no response, if any. However, there were dozens of POWs interested in the Army of Occupation, but that was not permitted under military regulations for obvious reasons. If any of these guys got back to Germany again, it would soon seem

"Hell's Belle" crew, September, 1988. *Left to right:* Gerald E. McDowell (author), Bert Stieler, Bill Rasmussen, Cecil Comer, Charles Dyer, Charles Guinn.

like there was a vigilante army in operation.

I got a train out of San Antonio to St. Louis and it seemed it was "clickety-clack" for three or more days just to get out of Texas. At St. Louis I caught the second section of the "Jeffersonian," an all-silver, shiny, high-speed through train to Philadelphia. It was high-speed alright; it came into Philadelphia around six hours late due to a pileup when we rammed the first section somewhere along the line and had to sit for hours. Fortunately no one was hurt, just shaken up a bit. This was on November 2 and with the tie-up, I didn't get into Philadelphia until sometime after 10:00 P.M., but I was home at last—to stay!

May the good Lord help me to never forget my gratitude for what I have endured and survived or the hardships of those eighteen months as a POW, nor the barbarians we had to deal with to make the world once again a free place to live!

D-Bar Values

This page shows how the various food items in our Red Cross parcels were valued according to the "D-Bar" in the package. This highly concentrated chocolate bar, found in each parcel, became our "monetary unit" and the basis for all trading. Exchange rate is shown below.

CONTENTS OF ONE R.C. PARCEL
(may vary)

	Trade Value
2 D-Bars	
1 can of instant coffee	(2 D-Bars)
1 one-pound can of powdered milk	(3 D-Bars)
1 box of lump sugar	(1 1/2 D-Bars)
1 eight-ounce Kraft cheese	(1 1/2 D-Bars)
1 "C" or "K" rations	(1 D-Bar)
1 tin of jam	(1 D-Bar)
1 pound tin of margarine	(1/2 D-Bar)
1 can of liver paste	(1/2 D-Bar)
5 packages of cigarettes	(1 D-Bar)

Cigarettes were about twenty cents a pack at that time and a D-Bar would buy eight packs. It was very rare to receive a popular brand cigarette. Those that came were off brands that we never heard of before and were a lousy smoke and very hard to trade, such as Twenty Grand and Domino.

The Last Days after Stalag 17-B

Stalag 17-B was a German POW camp located on top of a high hill at Krems, Austria, about forty miles northwest of Vienna. The camp consisted of 30,000 prisoners, 4,200 of which were Americans. The balance were Russians, Poles, Serbs, Italians, Czechs and other nationalities. The Americans were kept separate from the other prisoners. This was due to the forced labor for the others, but the Americans were not required to work under the regulations of the Geneva Convention due to their military rank.

Suddenly, on April 8, 1945, we were to be evacuated from the camp—all 4,200 of us. However, many had stayed behind because they could not walk, and others had bribed the guards so they could stay. We left in groups of five hundred, with about 15–20 minute intervals between groups. The six enlisted men from our crew had been there since December 1, 1943. It would not be until May 2, 1945, that we would be liberated in the town of Braunau, Germany, where Hitler was born. How ironic!

We covered 281 miles on this march, with only about eight guards to each group of five hundred Americans. That's how short of men the Germans were at this point, and they were all older men of the Wehrmacht at that and had trouble keeping up with us. We said nothing about the march to them as we headed steadily west, toward the Allies. Rations were in very short supply along the way. This was done on purpose so no one could save up food and attempt an escape from the group. Those who tried were apparently shot by roving guards following along, but well off the road, as we did hear shots ring out a few times after someone had disappeared. We marched in all kinds of weather: rain, snow, cold, etc. Being on the foothills of the Alps did not help any with the march or the weather. The snow was blinding at times, and one could only follow the feet of the man in front of him. There was no shelter at night. We all slept outdoors under the guard of machine guns. Only on two or three occasions did we get to sleep in a cow barn.

The following is from a log I kept during our 281-mile march from Krems to Braunau. The year was 1945.

SUNDAY—April 8

Evacuated Stalag 17-B at 11:00 A.M. in groups of 500. Rass, Windy, Charlie, and I left in the sixth group. We marched west until nearly dark. Slept on a hill near Stixendorf. Very tired and packs were heavy. Night was quite damp and cold—not much sleep. Could hear artillery fire in the distance and see flashes over the mountains. Covered about 30 kilometers today.

MONDAY—April 9

Broke camp about 12:30 P.M.. Not much marching, so we didn't cover much ground. A Jerry guard got Windy a canteen of wine someplace. We killed it about sundown. Windy also got some bread and eggs from a Jerry—boy, did they taste good after all these months (last eggs Nov. 1943). Moved up on a hill near Grossheindrickslag(?)— for the night. Tried to trade with a Kraut but "no dice." I hope Windy's "friend" continues to give us stuff. Got some chow. First since we left camp. A little barley and 1/18th of a loaf of bread. Not very cold tonight, I hope.

TUESDAY—April 10

Staying just outside of St. Johann all day today, so there isn't much of anything to write.

WEDNESDAY—April 11

Happy 22nd Birthday to me! Broke camp about 7:30 A.M. Stopped about an hour at Muhldorf. Covered 24 kilometers today. Stopped at Paggstall overnight. Had a stew of potatoes and some other crap. It was pretty good though—specially when you are hungry and marched all day and they only give you a small ladle of chow.

THURSDAY—April 12

Left Paggstall and marched to Altenmarkt. It started raining this morning. We covered 15 kilometers today. First night we've slept under shelter and that was only a cow shed. The Krauts said, "No more bread"—all gone I guess? Stumbled around in the dark getting chow (9:30 P.M.). Was very sick in the middle of the night. Not much sleep. It seems like dysentery, I'm so weak. No doubt I got whatever it is from some "bad" water I took out of a stream and didn't quite boil.

FRIDAY—April 13

Still felt sick this morning so the "Medics" let me put my pack on the wagon. Covered 13 kilometers today and it's still raining. I feel so weak after last night that I am just about ready to throw in the towel. Slept inside a paper-box mill. Very warm tonight. We had 3 small spuds and 1/15th of a loaf of bread that the GIs baked after our little Volkstrum Captain bought the flour and stuff along the road.

SATURDAY—April 14

Walked about a 1/2 a mile down the road for chow this morning. Had barley soup with meat. Got 2 small dippers this time—(big deal!). The Danube River is only 100 yards or so from where we just had our chow. I had always heard about the "beautiful blue" Danube, but it sure looks muddy to me! I was told it always looks like this.

According to a sign here, we are now 68 kilometers from Krems, but that it is by the main roads. The way we went is much farther. Shoved off for Grein about noon. Marched along the Danube all day, passing through the following towns: Hershenau, Sarmingstein, St. Nikola, and Struden. At Grein we slept in a barn. Got some hardtack and Schweitzer cheese. Covered 17 kilometers today.

SUNDAY—April 15

Left Grein for Klam. Marched 7 kilometers today. Slept in a building built in the 16th century. Got 6 hardtack biscuits and some boiled meat made into a watery soup.

MONDAY—April 16

Left this morning for Naarn. Marched through the following towns: Baumgartenberg and Mitterkirchen. Got 1/10th of loaf of bread and a small bag of hardtack biscuits that were made with caraway seeds (approx. 1/2 lb.). Got some very good barley soup, too! Covered about 23 kilometers today.

TUESDAY—April 17

Left Naarn for Steyregg. Passed through: Au on the Danube, Maluthausen, Langensteir, St. Georgea on the Gusen, and Pulgarn. Town was bombed last night. Heading for Linz tomorrow. Covered 23 kilometers today. Had cornmeal soup with meat and 1/9th of a loaf of bread, plus 2 dippers of soup.

WEDNESDAY—April 18

Marched through Linz and Plesching and Wilhering. Stayed 5 kilometers outside of Wilhering. Knocked off 17 kilometers today with only one 15 minute break. The reason was to get through Linz as quickly as possible because it was a vital area and being hit day and night. Had barley soup and three spuds for chow. Webb gave me his barley, so I'll cook it up for chow tomorrow morning. Made 31 kilometers today.

THURSDAY—April 19

Left for Horsdof. Passed through: Alkoven, Strass-Emling, and Fraham. Had some canned meat, and 9 men shared 1/2 lb. of margarine, 1 tablespoon of coffee, 1/2 tablespoon of sugar, and 1/5th of a 2# loaf of bread. Slept inside a barn. Covered 15 kilometers. The Protective Power and the Red Cross visited us and said they would try to get us some parcels.

FRIDAY—April 20

Headed for Kallham. Passed through: Kalkafen, Daxberg, Michaelnvach, Patting, Widldorf, and Newmarkt. Laid over 14 hours. Received Red Cross parcels. We had 4 types of them so we cut cards for choice. I cut the King of Diamonds (second choice), so took a Canadian parcel and boy it was "prima!" The other choices were American, French, and American Invalid. Rass and Charlie went scrounging around and they picked up 18 eggs, 2/3 of a kilo of bread, 1/4 lb. of bacon, and 1 kilo of spuds. This cost Charlie his sweater he got from home and a shave stick, plus 1/2 pack of cigarettes. Covered 26 kilometers today. Had 2 meals, both milky cornbread. No bread today.

SUNDAY—April 22

Headed for Eitzing. Passed through: Erlach, Riedau, Petersham, Taiskirchen, Andrichfurt, and Aurolzmunster. Had watery pea soup at Aurolzmunster and 1/5th of kilo of bread. Finished march to Eitzing. Slept in a barn. Made 26 kilometers today.

MONDAY—April 23

Started for Altheim. Passed through: Mairing, Ranzing, Gurten, Ornading, Imolkan, and Polling. No chow tonight! Slept in a barn 2 kilometers from Altheim. Made 24 kilometers today.

TUESDAY—April 24

Got a 24 hour layover today. Rass rounded up a little oleo, bread, 6 eggs, and 200 saccharine tablets.

I bought 5 kilos of spuds from the guards for a package of Prince Albert. For chow we had a double ration of barley soup (slightly thinned) and 1/7th of a kilo of bread.

WEDNESDAY—April 25

Headed for Braunau. Marched 23 kilometers today. Wound up in a woods well up on a large hill 10 kilometers from Braunau. Passed through: Elling, St Peter, Braunau, and Ranshofen to get the top of this hill. We are told this is the destination. Our "combine" built a lean-to of pine boughs and poles cut from tree limbs, also made a bedding of pine boughs. Comer joined us, so now the 5 of us are sleeping together. No chow tonight. Tomorrow we get 3/4th's of a "Frog" parcel per man. We have come over 300 kilometers (281 miles) from Krems.

This Is a More Complete List of the Towns We Went Through in the Forced March across Austria

Krems
Renburg
Senftenburg
Ludendorf
Himberg
Muhldorf
Freistitz
Heiligeblut
Streitrofesen
Poggstall
Laimbach
Hirschenau
Isperdorf
Sarmingsten
St. Nikola
Stamden
Grein
Klamm
Baumgartenburg
Mitterkirchen
Naarn
Au
Mouthousen
St. Georgen
Lufttenberg
Steyregg
Plesching
Linz
(crossed Danube River here)
Wilhecing

Alkoven
Fraham
Horsling
St. Thomas
Prambachkirchen
Michaelbach
Potting
Neumarkt
Widldorf
Kallham
Erlach
Riedau
Taiskirchen
Anolrichsfust
Aurolzmunster
Eitzing
Mairing
Ranzing
Surten
Freiling
Seinberg
Durtcham
Altheim
St. Peter
Haselbach
Braunau
Randshafen
Inn-Salzuch Blick
(in woods, war was over;
   rain, cold as hell!)

THURSDAY—April 26

First day in camp, if you want to call it that! Red Cross trucks around with parcels, all French. Parcels were given 3 to 4 men. Jerry gave us 4 teaspoons of barley, 1/18th of a 2-kilo loaf of bread, and four raw spuds.

FRIDAY—April 27

Clear today. Jerry gave us 3 teaspoons of dry millet, 1/2 teaspoon of butter, 2 small raw spuds, no bread! Red Cross parcels came in today.

SATURDAY—April 28

Rained last night and all day today. Had 1 1/2 ounces of Jerry hardtack, 1/2 teaspoon of salt, 2 tablespoons of dry barley, 1/2 teaspoon of butter—no bread again!

SUNDAY—April 29

Rained almost all night and off and on today. Had 2 tablespoons of dry rolled oats, 1/2 teaspoon of salt, 1/2 teaspoon of butter, and 4 uncooked spuds. No bread. Received 1 American and 1 British parcel for each 4 men. These are supposed to be *1 full parcel per man!*

MONDAY—April 30

Rained off and on all day today. Had 1 teaspoon of butter, 1 1/2 teaspoons of white beans, 2 tablespoons of barley. No bread!

TUESDAY—May 1

Rained again today. Had 5 raw spuds, 1 tablespoon of white beans. This afternoon Sid Hall got orders to give out every bit of chow in the kitchen because American tanks were very near Braunau, so we later got 1 tablespoon of ersatz coffee, 1 1/2 tablespoons of white beans, 1 teaspoon of salt, 1/5th of a pound of meat, 3 teaspoons of dry barley, but no bread. From up on the hill the mess area overlooked the Inn River. We could see a couple of half-tracks, some jeeps, and a number of tanks (American) coming up the valley on the other side of the river. I wonder what tomorrow will bring?

WEDNESDAY—May 2

Rained again today. No rations. This was the happiest day since we left the States. An American spearhead took Braunau this morning, which is only 10 kilometers from here. The captain in command came here under truce and talked to us. As the story goes, the Jerry colonel wanted to surrender his staff, himself, and us to the Yanks. The first words that came out of the captain's mouth, as he climbed up on a tree stump nearby, were—"Men you are no longer POWs, but soldiers of the United States Army!" This was at 7:20 P.M.

THURSDAY—May 3

This morning the 13th Armored Division moved in and officially took over the camp. They took the Jerry guards prisoner and started to make arrangements for moving us out and supplying us with food. Our food supplies are entirely gone.

FRIDAY—May 4

Rained all day. Had 1/5th of a 2 kilo loaf of bread, 2 tablespoons of beans, 1 tablespoon of salt, 1 pound of flour, and a 1/4 pound of meat. Army rations haven't caught up with the advance force yet. The above rations were confiscated from Jerry towns. We did receive 1 thick slice of white bread also. This ration was small only because the number of trucks to haul food was limited and there were too many men to feed. Gradually there will be enough chow.

SATURDAY—May 5

As usual it rained today. The Army and some of our appointed men confiscated more food. Received 1/4 pound of rice, 2 pounds of flour, 1/4 pound of Jerry coffee, 1 pound of sugar, and 12 eggs for 25 men. Army "K" rations came in so each man got a B, D, and an S unit. We had a few "gash" rations so we cut cards for them, and I got an extra D unit. The battalion commander had men out confiscating food. They brought in 63 eggs per 25 men and a lot of other stuff, including some apples, which was my first taste of apples in 2 years. At 7:10 P.M. we marched up the road 10 miles to Ranshofen to an aluminum factory for some decent shelter—we have been outside nearly every night since April 24.

SUNDAY—May 6

Boy, it was nice to sleep inside where it was warm and dry, even though it was a hard floor—cement. Received 1/3 of a loaf of American white bread and Army rations type "C." Boy talk about that thing they call *"eat!"* Also, moved into better quarters.

MONDAY—May 7

Was a little sick last night due to the change of diet, I guess. Today we were given 2 pounds of sugar and 2 kilos of spuds. Late this afternoon we received orders to move out. Rass and Charlie went to the USO show and none of us (Comer, Wingate, or I) had time to go for them, so they were left behind. We were put on half-tracks and headed for Passau, where we stopped at an airport. We are sleeping out tonight because the planes have not come in yet. Received another Army type "C" ration. We are at Tutting Airfield, which is near Potting on the north side of the Inn River, also near Shondorf.

TUESDAY—May 8

Beautiful day today. Had breakfast of cereal, coffee, and "C" biscuits. Transports started to arrive at about 9:00 A.M.. We sat around until 5:00 P.M. waiting for enough planes to arrive to take us out. We took off at 5:10 for Epinal. While we were waiting for the C-47s, a Jerry transport came in and surrendered the ship, crew, and everything. There was a crew of 4 plus 2 Luftwaffe women. I ran out and jumped up on the back of the truck they were put on. Confronting one Kraut, I took a handmade swastika from his tunic. A buddy who had a knife cut it loose for me.

The Kraut was a Navy man, I think. It was an impressive decoration with a copper-colored wreath around the swastika and the usual colors they use on such things. It was apparently important to him, judging by they way he carried on to keep it. We soon took off after this incident and later landed at Nancy, France, at 7:15 P.M. The French "civies" were at the airport to greet us as we landed. Then we took GI trucks to the center of town and they fed us a good old GI meal in a GI mess hall, diner style. A French combo played "The Stars and Stripes Forever" as we ate. After this, we took trucks down to the railroad station and boarded box-cars, World War I vintage of the old 40/8, to Epinal. It was rough riding and I couldn't sleep, but I didn't care. Arrived at Epinal around 5:00 A.M.

WEDNESDAY—May 9

We headed for the RAMP (Recovered Allied Military Personnel) camp reception center at Epinal. There they gave us a talk on how we would be taken care of here and there until we reached the States and got our *60-day furlough*. We then were assigned to barracks, got 2 blankets and mess gear. At 6:00 A.M. we went to mess and had cheese sandwiches and coffee while we waited for breakfast time. The food here will be carefully controlled by a dietician over a period of 7 to 10 days, depending how fast each man responds. There are three mess halls,

145

starting with the first room, which is bland food with no seasoning. Gradually the food is brought back to a "normal" level as you go from one room to the next, usually two or three days apart.

Later I went over to the PX and got weekly rations of: 2 cigars, 7 pks. of cigarettes, 5 Hershey bars, 2 pks. of gum, 1 toothbrush, 1 tube of shaving cream, 1 pkg. of razor blades and a bar of soap. This was a complimentary issue. Just took it easy the rest of the day. I saw a lot of Kraut POWs and boy does it do my heart good to see those dirty Nazis do a little work. First time I have been able to sleep with my socks off since last winter.

THURSDAY—May 10

Awoke about 7:45 A.M. and went to chow. Had scrambled eggs, white bread, oatmeal, grapefruit juice, and coffee. Noon chow was good also: beef, carrots, mashed potatoes, etc. Had showers at 4:00 P.M. Issued new O.D. shirt and pants, razor and 5 blades, new cap, new combat boots, field jacket, sleeping bag, raincoat, etc. I got a ride into town with a colonel from the camp. I can't speak any French, so I figured that Epinal is no place for me. One of the boys from Stalag 17-B that I knew very well has a brother (Bill Caruso) here driving the truck that I came back in. It was 10:00 P.M. when I got back so I walked over to the Red Cross club and had 3 dishes of ice cream. I had a bottle of Coke this morning and a dish of ice cream. We were told we could leave as soon as we got our delousing and clothes, so Windy, Comer, and I are going out on the first convoy in the morning.

FRIDAY—May 11

Had breakfast then packed up and jumped on the convoy to the station. As soon as we were settled on the train we got coffee, bread, and a can of "C" type rations. The "C" rations will continue for the rest of the trip.

SATURDAY—May 12

Didn't sleep hardly at all last night, sitting up in this day coach all night. Just passed the time away reading, eating, and walking around each time we stopped for a while. Reached a station about 40 miles from Le Havre and transferred to trucks. From here we rode about 4 or 5 miles to a place called "Camp Lucky Strike." Got in line and signed up for a furlough to come when we hit the USA. Went to chow about 1:30 A.M. Had stewed chicken, mashed potatoes, applesauce, 4 slices of bread, and coffee. By the time chow was over I got in the "sack" as it was nearly 3:00 A.M. We are sleeping in large tents, approximately 25 men per tent.

SUNDAY—May 13

Slept very well last night. Didn't wake up until 10:00 A.M., then Arthur Shroyer and I went over to the R.C. and had an eggnog. It was the most delicious one I have ever tasted. It had nutmeg and all.

They didn't serve any breakfast. Went over to the canteen and had another eggnog. Also, sent a wire home to tell them I had been liberated. Met a fella named Earl Forte who lives only 2 blocks from me on City Line Ave. Ate supper then went over to the R.C. for a sandwich, but it was closed. Nothing doing so I hit the sack. Pretty cold tonight.

MONDAY—May 14

Had chow then went for an eggnog. Waiting to be processed now. Ate noon chow then laid down and smoked a cigar. Nothing doing tonight so Earl, Art, and I walked over to the R.C. and had a cup of cocoa and cheese sandwich. We tried to get in to see a show but it was too crowded, so we went back and hit the sack.

TUESDAY—May 15

No chow this morning. About noon we went for our medical exam. We got our second meal about midnight. Not feeling so good so I went to bed.

WEDNESDAY—May 16

Ate breakfast then sat around waiting for PX rations (complimentary). Comer told me where I could find Lt. Fallek, so I looked around till I did. From the PX we got 7 pks. of "butts" (L.S. and Camels), a comb, shaving cream, razor blades, 14 ounce can of tomato juice, 1 pkg. of gum, box of Kleenex (for 3 men), a toothbrush, a pencil, 1 Air Mail tablet. Then we cut cards for the mirrors, sewing kits, pipe tobacco, and shoe polish. We should get towels later. —Just got two towels!

THURSDAY—May 17

Still nothing doing. All we do is "sweat out" the chow line then sit down and wait for the next meal. Went out and got a haircut then after the noon meal went for a shower along with Harry Davis. Nothing doing, so I went to evening chow then hit the sack.

FRIDAY—May 18

Ate breakfast then as usual just sat around. After dinner I started a letter. I was stumped for words after having been a POW for so long. I finally finished it about supper time.

I ran into Charles Clark and he was just shipping out so he gave me 80 fr. ($1.60).

Walked over to the PX in "D" area but it was closed.

Saw Gilbert Taft, he was leaving.

Got 19 eggs from the mess hall, then hit the sack.

SATURDAY—May 19

Today makes a week we've been here. I walked over to the PX 3 times today, and it was closed every time!

Boiled 18 eggs and ate a couple while I waited for chow.

Had another eggnog this afternoon—PRIMA!

Wrote a letter home this evening.

Nothing doing so I hit the sack.

It rained!

SUNDAY—May 20

Had chow then went to see Windy right after our Air Corps meeting. Earl Forte and I walked over to the PX and I bought us each a cigarette case and a big jackknife for myself. Davis and I went to the R.C. for cocoa. Ate chow then hit the sack.

It's raining again, or rather still!

MONDAY—May 21

Got PX rations: 7 pkgs. of L.S. & Camels, 2 boxes of matches, 1 can of Phillips tomato juice (14 ounces), five razor blades, 1 pkg. of gum, and 1 bar of Sweetheart soap.

It rained all afternoon so we didn't go for our processing.

TUESDAY—May 22

Pulled C.Q. this afternoon.

Not much doing until Gen. Eisenhower came in on a C-47 to look the place over.

Went for clothes at 3:00 P.M. Got three full suits of sun tans, 4 handkerchiefs, 3 prs. of socks, a new battle blouse, new O.D. pants, dog-tag chain, belt, fatigue cap, O.D. cap, O.D. shirt, and a new type barracks bag.

There was an accident in R.C. this evening.

Rained this afternoon.

WEDNESDAY—May 23
      You guessed it, rain again!
      Nothing to do all day except read. I'm reading "Beat to Quarters" by C.S. Forester.
      Went to Air Corps meeting after chow. Had information lecture by a Lt. Col. Smith from A.A.F. headquarters, Washington, D.C.

THURSDAY—May 24
      Got some of our ribbons and "H" (Hersey) bars for our uniforms.
      Expect to move out tonight.
      Had an eggnog, shot darts, then read until we left for "D" area about 12:00 P.M.

FRIDAY—May 25
      Went through interrogation, physical, and other processing, and then got a typhus shot, ouch!
      Everything seems like a mad rush to fill out this and sign that, also got dog tags.
      Had noon chow.
      Signed up for a few more campaign ribbons and battle stars.
      Went to the R.C. and had two eggnogs with Earl Forte and another fellow.
      Came back and hit the "sack." Quite cold tonight.

SATURDAY—May 26
      Nothing doing this morning except PX rations. I didn't need the other stuff so I just took the matches, gum, and cigarettes.
      Expect to be paid this afternoon.
      Rained a little.
      No pay!, so Earl Forte and I went to the outdoor movie. We saw the "Merry Monahans."

SUNDAY—May 27

Had breakfast then sat around until pay call which didn't come until after dinner. We got 2,500 Fr. ($50.00).

Went over to the PX but the line was too long.

Earl and I had a catch for a while, then we played some Ping-Pong.

Expect to move out tonight.

Left "D" area and moved over to "A" block.

MONDAY—May 28

After breakfast Earl and I went over to the PX. We went into the gift shop and bought some French perfume and cologne, a cigarette lighter, and a wallet. The GI in charge explained how the perfume being minus all the duties and taxes could be sold through the government to Ex-POWs much cheaper. It was selling for 1/5th the price it would cost in the U.S.

Cigarette lighter	Fr. 43
Wallet	Fr. 100
2 bottles of Perfume	Fr. 488
2 bottles of Cologne	Fr. 52
	Fr. 683 ($13.66)

Later in the afternoon we went over to the R.C., had 2 eggnoggs, then we sat and filled our lighters.

Later in the evening I saw part of a USO show.

About 10:30 P.M.. I saw an outdoor movie called "Mr. Winkle Goes to War," with Edward G. Robinson.

TUESDAY—May 29

(No notes kept from here until 6/12/45. I don't know why!)

TUESDAY—June 5

Shoved off for the old USA and HOME!

TUESDAY—June 12

Arrived on U.S. soil. Been processed, clothed, and paid. Now I'm just waiting to get home!